WEEKEND

First published in 1990 by Third House (Publishers)
69, Regent Street, Exeter, EX 2 9 EG

Copyright Martin Foreman 1990

Reprinted 1991

ISBN I 870188 15 2

Typeset by Rapid Communications Ltd., Bristol, BS3 1DX
Printed by Billing & Sons, Ltd., Worcester
Distributed in the United Kingdom and in Western Europe
by Turnaround Distribution Co-op, Ltd.,
27, Horsell Road, London, N5 1XL

Distributed in the United States of America
by Inland Book Company, 254, Bradley Street, East Haven,
Connecticut, 06512, U.S.A.
and Bookpeople, 2929, Fifth Street, Berkeley, California, 94710, U.S.A.

Distributed in Australia and New Zealand
by Stilone Pty. Ltd., P.O. Box 155, Broadway,
New South Wales 2007, Australia

Cover picture: Mike Ferrari

WEEKEND

Martin Foreman

THIRD HOUSE (PUBLISHERS)

For those who were
Robert, Carl and Gene

But life don't clickety-clack
Down a straight-line track
It comes together and it comes apart
—*Ferron*

ONE

Mark was woken from a warm and comfortable dream by the distant sounds of Ben in the kitchen. Once recognised, the vague noises that resolved into the clatter of cutlery and plates ceased to disturb him and he shifted position slightly as if stretching out, letting his toes curl over the foot of the mattress and half-smothering his face in the crook of an arm, would allow him to slip more easily back into sleep. He was held back, however, by a dense and grey emotion, a deep, almost painful regret which hovered like a low dark cloud that threatened to become at any moment damp and unwelcome rain.

For a few minutes Mark lay, his thoughts as motionless as his body, knowing that even the slightest effort to recapture sleep would only frighten it away. The world receded; sounds became fainter. Light faded into dark and touch melted but his consciousness, instead of dissipating, focused on the cloud, saw it slowly take shape, resolve into Robert's features, his look of hurt and accusation, his words of disappointment, his refusal to be kissed or even touched by Mark as he walked away.

As if to sweep away the memory, Mark turned over and opened his eyes for no longer than was necessary to read the bedside clock. In doing so he saw that he had not only woken disagreeably early for a Saturday morning but that his room was filled with a summer light that London, and Mark, seldom knew. The attraction of sunshine, warmth and clear skies on a day when he did not have to teach, however, was weaker than that of sleep, and he turned onto his side, withdrew his head beneath the covers and hugged the pillow as he would have hugged Robert, as

1

he had hugged Carl and Gene and others before them. The action was as momentarily satisfactory as a reflex, but the pillow's softness, its smallness, its lack of smell and resistance, soon irritated and he pushed it away.

Surrendering, Mark reached out a hand and switched on the radio. The bright and jaunty music dragged him gently awake while the cheerful voice of the presenter conveying a bland message of love from one unknown listener to another was reassuring, as if hidden in his words or tone was the promise of a prosperous and propitious future. Mark felt life and strength return to his body and limbs and he opened his eyes to acknowledge that he was at last fully awake. Pushing himself up to a half-sitting position he looked round as if almost expecting a knock on the door and a bell-hop to enter, carrying a silver tray with orange juice, coffee and the other trappings of breakfast.

With consciousness, however, came memory and as the images and words of the previous evening flowed back, so the sunshine which had saturated the room with optimism seemed suddenly dull, colourless, a pledge of joy and happiness that would never be fulfilled. It was as if he had awoken not only from the previous night's sleep but from the last three months, and the growing happiness he had felt had been no more real than the morning's dream which had already faded from his mind. He would, he knew, see Robert again; they would go out together, perhaps even sleep together as before, but he was no longer sure, as he had been twelve hours earlier, that their relationship would continue to develop, that their love would broaden and deepen.

He pushed back the duvet, stood up and went over to pick up one by one the pile of clothes that lay on the chair, less conscious of his actions than of the conversation of the previous night. As he pulled on underwear and jeans and searched through a drawer for a clean tee-shirt, he tried to understand why his initial and righteous feelings of hurt had diminished into guilt and sifted through Robert's words for any indication that the cut was not deep, that it was only Robert's vanity and not his self-respect that had been wounded. The only conclusion Mark came to, however, was that his ineptitude and self-centredness had all but destroyed everything that he was eager and impatient to build.

He could remember every word, not of the earlier part of the evening, their banter as they walked up Tottenham Court Road to the Indian restaurant behind Euston Station, nor later their intensity as they talked for what seemed like hours over the puri, dhosa and kulfi, but the end, when it had all begun to fall apart, when Robert had asked in the occasionally formal manner that in others would have seemed ridiculous but in him appeared perfectly natural, 'Can I ask you something?' And Mark had known what the 'thing' was, had, foolishly, he now realised, thought it buried and forgotten, unaware that it had merely stood patiently aside, waiting for the moment when, undisturbed by pressures of time or place, it could reappear.

'Sure,' he said, his expression and tone suggesting a confidence and ease he did not feel.

'Why did you take back that tape?' The tape that Mark had made of his songs, the tape that he hoped would take him out of teaching with its indifferent pupils and its petty politics and disputes and into the music world, into the world itself, the tape he had taken back three days before, lifting it from Robert's bag in a moment of anger and wounded pride.

'Because I didn't think you were interested in it.'

Robert looked at him for a moment as if he had not understood what Mark had said. 'But I asked you for it. I've been waiting for weeks to listen to it. And you just took it away before I had a chance. Without even telling me. Why? Don't you trust me?'

He stared at Mark, his dark eyes cold beneath the mass of black hair that covered his brow, his lips straight, sealed, almost bitter.

'Of course I trust you,' Mark said, 'but after Tuesday night I thought you'd lost interest in me. I didn't want you to hear the tape; it was too personal, too private.'

'Tuesday? When I went out with the Merrivales? What about it?'

3

'You didn't invite me.' In the coldness of their conversation the accusation sounded ridiculous, childish, an excess of pride, of amour propre.

'You'd said you were busy. You had exams or something to correct. Anyway, you don't know them; you're hardly ever likely to meet them again. Why should I invite you?'

It seemed so obvious to Mark that he wondered for a moment if Robert was being wilfully blind. 'Because we see so little of each other. Time is precious. And I'd like to get to know your friends.'

'I saw you the same day. When you took back the tape. Without telling me. Before I had a chance to listen to it.' They had met upstairs in McDonald's in Oxford Street; Robert had casually mentioned going out the evening before. Later, he had gone to the toilet and Mark, after watching him disappear as he always watched Robert, every movement, every action he made, had leaned over and searched in his bag, pushing aside the towels and sweat-ridden leotards, finding the tape, stuffing it into his jacket pocket before Robert could return. He said nothing, sure that that night, after looking for the tape in his turn and discovering it missing, Robert would be shamed into understanding the pain Mark had felt.

'That was only for half an hour. Anyway, you'd had the tape for three days and hadn't listened to it.'

'Because I hadn't had time. I wanted to sit down with plenty of time to listen to it carefully, to understand what you're trying to do. Now there's no point – it seems you don't trust me.'

'Of course I do.' Mark's heart sank. He had imagined the scene differently, imagined Robert admitting his thoughtlessness, his guilt, apologising for hurting Mark's feelings as Mark generously brushed the incident aside and handed back the tape in a gesture of reconciliation. Now all the reasons that had seemed at the time so important, so meaningful, so justified, were little more than excuses, weak attempts to cover the fact that he had behaved stupidly and selfishly. Their positions were reversed and Mark's just punishment was

4

now seen as the crime. 'I was just upset by Tuesday night.'

'And I've explained. I saw no reason for you to come along. I thought you'd be bored.'

'I'm never bored with you.' He sounded insincere or, just as bad, naive.

Robert said nothing and yet that was surely the point – they should never be bored with each other, never assume that one would rather be alone. Mark was in the right – at least about Tuesday – but he had not been able to make himself understood. Now, as a result of that failure they were staring at each other over the remains of their meal, the half-drunk coffee, the empty wine glasses, Robert's expression unchanged, almost hostile, devoid of all the warmth and enthusiasm of the earlier part of the evening.

'I'll give you the tape back on Sunday.'

'What's the point?'

'Just listen to it, please.' They were the wrong words, the wrong tone. He was indeed pleading, a sign of weakness, the one defect that Robert would not accept.

Robert shrugged. 'If you like.'

Although he knew it would be better to keep silent, to show indifference, to pretend that he didn't care and thus maintain the fiction of his strength of character, what Mark needed most of all at that moment was to have Robert display some desire, some eagerness to hear his tape, the sixty minutes of Mark at the piano with a backing group singing his own songs. While part of him screamed shut up, you're crawling, you're making things worse, he went on, 'I really want you to listen to it.'

Robert only shrugged again. 'I said I don't see the point.'

They were silent again. Robert sat at an angle, watching him with the same intense stare. Mark read pity there and sorrow and was angered because he was the older one, the more adult; those emotions were his right. 'What does this mean for us?' he asked.

'I don't know,' Robert said, lack of interest in his tone. 'I'm feeling hurt. I don't know how I'll feel tomorrow or when we see each other again.'

5

What about my hurt, Mark wondered but could not ask. It had been his stupidity, his childish need for revenge that had created this scene. 'Can't we talk about it now?' he asked, again aware of and hating the begging in his voice.

'No.' Robert looked for the waiter, signed to him to bring the bill. Mark became aware of the restaurant again, the other tables and customers; they were no more real than a stage backdrop.

'When are you coming back?' he asked after a pause, his tone almost cheerful.

'I told you. Sunday evening.'

'What time?'

'I don't know. The performance'll end about nine o'clock. Then it depends if the others want to stay for a couple of drinks.'

'Give me a call when you come back.'

'Maybe.'

The waiter, a middle-aged man either bored or expecting no tip, handed Robert the bill. He looked at it and handed it without a word to Mark. When both had counted their money and put it on the table, Robert said, 'Shall we go?'

'So soon?'

'I have to get up early. I want a good night's sleep.'

An excuse. It did not matter that Mark had known for some time that Robert's company had two dates booked in the Midlands, that Mark had expected to sleep that weekend, as he slept each week, alone; all he heard from Robert was a deliberately feeble excuse.

'Robert,' he said as they stood up and pulled on their jackets, 'I'm sorry.'

'So am I.'

He watched Robert's back as they walked out into the street, the worn black jacket muffling the broad shoulders and the body that he had learned to appreciate with not only a lover's but a choreographer's eye. He was losing something wonderful, something his thoughtlessness had simply tossed away. There was nothing he could do to regain it except hope and wait. Perhaps the whole incident would be forgotten when Robert returned. Perhaps

6

Robert would understand what Mark had felt. Perhaps, perhaps.

'I'm going to catch my bus,' Robert said.

'I'll walk you to the stop.'

'It's all right; I'd rather go alone.' The end of three months' tradition standing by a darkened shop, shifting from one foot to the other, making weak jokes, talking about nothing and talking about everything as they waited for the tall narrow vehicle to come. At first Mark had resented the fact that Robert had to go home, that he still lived with a mother who was unhappy about his dancing, who wished not so much to control as to observe her son's life, until he imbued these partings with their own romance and persuaded himself that it would not be a good idea for them to sleep together too much too soon. Now it seemed that even these bitter-sweet minutes were denied him.

'O.K.' Where was the magic word or phrase that would obliterate the last half-hour, that would restore all the feelings that both had held before? 'Break a leg,' he smiled, 'both of them.' He leaned forward to kiss but Robert had moved away.

'Thanks.' The expression was cold. 'I'll call you.'

Mark watched the figure walk away slowly, the bag, as ever, slung over his shoulder. His slow, slightly bow-legged gait seemed to express all the sorrow that both of them felt, Robert at Mark's lack of feeling, Mark at his own stupidity. He waited, hoping that Robert would look round, see him standing there, be so overcome with love and remorse that he would run back and almost knock him over with his embrace, but all that Mark saw was the man he needed turn the corner as if he did not exist, as if the evening, all the time they had known each other, had never taken place. Shivering, not sure whether he was about to cry, Mark turned back and started walking towards the underground station.

After that there had been nothing; a tube journey he did not remember, the short and familiar walk through the streets of Clapham to his front door, an hour anaesthetised by an old film on television and the night's sleep from

7

which he had just awoken. Now he was in the bathroom, flushing the toilet and perfunctorily washing the sleep from his eyes while Robert was having breakfast or had perhaps already left, was sitting in the hired minibus, laughing and joking with the others as they drove north, absorbed once again in his world, the world of dance, having forgotten Mark as Mark was incapable of forgetting him.

Ben was still in the kitchen, *The Times* spread out on the table in front of him, dirty dishes pushed to one side. He greeted Mark with a friendliness that bordered on the polite and both were relieved when conversation went no further, allowing Mark to prepare his breakfast and Ben to return to his newspaper. Mark neither liked nor disliked his lodger, having chosen him to replace Carl for the dependable and non-descript impression he had made when he came to look at the room. A recent graduate, who had carefully chosen his first job as the first step in what he promised himself would be a successful career, and who was equally carefully trawling the bars and lonely hearts columns for the appropriate professional male to accompany him on his upward path, Ben represented for Mark, depending on the mood he was in, either the epitome of a cold and calculating world that he was glad to be little part of or the symbol of self-confidence and determination that he himself lacked. They seldom saw each other, however, and for most of the time Ben was little more than a welcome supplement to Mark's income and the occasional irritation of unwashed dishes and noisily closed doors.

By the time Mark had made coffee and toast and decided first in favour and then against cooking bacon and eggs, Ben had cleared up and gone back to his room. Mark sat, poured cereal into a bowl and noticed again how strong and clear the sunlight was, how it threw each object it fell upon into relief, how it suddenly made the kitchen – and therefore the world – different, as if it was revealing another dimension, one that was not physical, but emotional, experiential, one that waited as inviting and easy to enter as Alice's mirror. There, it seemed,

8

through the turbulence of his emotions he saw an inner strength and peace, the person he might have been, the person he might yet be. The sensation was not new and would not last, but it was as intoxicating as it was delicate and he sat silent, motionless, until it dissolved into the warmth of another day.

The sun had shone as brightly, although it had been mid-autumn and its warmth was hollow, on the morning when Mark had woken, not sprawled across the bed as usual, but with his legs drawn up and a hand resting on the hip of the body beside him. He remembered the previous night, bringing Carl to bed and the awkward-ness which had faded but not died completely. His eyes flickered open; he saw the back of Carl's head with its long blond hair sprayed over the pillow and the vulnerable pallor of his skin. He thought about reaching over, kissing the back of Carl's neck, gently putting his hand round Carl's waist and pulling him into the warmth of his own body, but was afraid to do so, was afraid to worsen a position already compromised. Not that he regretted the previous night, but he did not know how to behave from now on.

As he lay undecided, Carl suddenly stretched, turned and opened his eyes. 'Morning,' he smiled.

'Morning.'

'What time is it?' His voice was quiet, little more than a whisper.

Mark turned, looked at the clock. 'Ten past eight.'

'Too early,' Carl muttered, closing his eyes and pulling himself up against Mark so that his forehead rested on Mark's collar-bone and an arm was draped round his waist. The renewed proximity abruptly dispelled Mark's doubts; reticence was senseless when such moments were so rare. He drew Carl even closer, looked down and kissed the rumpled hair, felt the roughness of his body against his own and let his hand seek the warmth and hardness in Carl's groin.

It's a beautiful day, he told himself as he waited for the kettle to boil and the toast to turn brown under the grill.

The leaves on the tree outside the kitchen window had turned gold and red, but had not yet been spilled to the ground by an impatient wind. School and its problems were a distant memory; the day stretched before him like a new country to explore. He heard the bathroom door open and Carl pad back into the bedroom. In a few minutes he would come in and they would sit down to breakfast. Mark wondered briefly how they would behave towards each other; they had hardly had time to adjust to being landlord and lodger. Last night had been a mistake but he was not yet sure whether it was one to regret.

'You're not working tonight?' he had asked as the programme they were watching gave way to advertisements.

Carl shook his head. 'Day off.'

'Do you always have Friday off?' The three days since Carl had moved in had told Mark little of his routine.

'No. Depends on the rota. It changes each week.' Carl had a northern accent that from time to time made itself easily heard.

'What's the place like?'

'Ewings? It's O.K. Better than some I've worked in.'

A bartender, Mark had said to himself when Carl came to look at the room. Why not? You might get free drinks. It had been a disappointment to learn that most of Carl's customers were free-spending salesmen and their heavily made-up girlfriends. 'Wouldn't you rather work somewhere gay?'

Carl frowned, as if he were making an effort to remember something. 'I don't know. I don't think the tips would be so good. And there'd be all the competition, all the customers trying to pick me up.'

'I'd be flattered,' Mark said. And so, he thought, should Carl, who had all the attributes of a handsome actor, fair hair that floated across his brow, blue eyes that held Mark each time he looked into them, an attractively sullen expression which without warning would break into a childishly pleasing smile. It was those good looks which had persuaded Mark to give Carl the room and which he had been trying for three days to ignore.

10

They were silent for a few moments, watching the images on the screen.

'Don't you have homework to do?' Carl asked.

'I'm a teacher, not a pupil.'

'I mean books to correct or something like that.'

Carl looked offended; Mark felt guilty and softened his tone. 'I try to get it all done at school and bring home as little as possible. When I'm not actually in the building I like to forget I've got anything to do with it.'

'I hated school too.'

'But teachers are supposed to be dedicated. Live, breathe and sleep school. Some of them do. Some of them spend hours on the kids or union affairs. All I want to do is take the money and run.'

'Why not find another job?'

'I'm trying.'

'What as?'

Mark never knew how to express himself in a way that was neither too modest or proud. 'I write songs.'

'Oh.' Carl showed mild curiosity where Mark had hoped for enthusiasm. 'What kind?'

'Love songs. Songs about life.'

'Any I'd know?'

Each time Mark heard that question his ego took another knock, for it implied that if his work wasn't sung, wasn't known, it was worthless and he was only trying to fool others and maybe himself in claiming to be a songwriter. 'No. I've sold a couple,' he added, trying to redeem himself, 'but they've never been recorded.'

'How come?'

'I don't know.' But he did know. He had sold them simply to be able to say that someone had been interested enough in his work to buy it, even though he had known that the company had been no more than one woman and a telephone, that she had had no more firm contacts in the music world than he had. It had almost been worth it, however, to hear his work being praised, to hear her say that she was sure X or Y would be interested, even though he well knew his songs were far removed from their style.

11

'So that's what the piano's for,' Carl said, as if the presence of the instrument had been a mystery to him. 'Will you play one for me?'

'I'm not in the mood,' he said. 'Another time.' When he knew that Carl's request was not merely curious or polite, when his confidence in his own ability was flowing not ebbing, when it did not matter whether Carl was able to recognise whatever talent Mark might have.

'O.K.' Carl said in a voice so quiet and accepting that it was almost as disturbing as if he had shouted.

The programme had restarted, but neither paid it any attention. Mark found himself staring at Carl, at the half-sad eyes and open expression. He wanted Carl, as much as he had wanted the figure who had rung his doorbell three days before, but it was as wrong to abuse the situation as a drunk, knowing that Carl was trapped behind his bar, might persist in trying to pick him up. Yet, as he looked at Carl, he was sure he saw the reflection of his own desire, the suggestion that Carl would give himself, was willing to make love, if Mark could only find the right words, the approach that was neither too crass nor too subtle.

'You should be a model,' Mark said. 'I mean the real thing – fashion, advertisements.'

'No way.' Carl took the words at face value rather than the compliment that had been intended. 'I've known a couple. They all think they're better than everyone else and they're just more stupid.'

'You'd make a fortune. You've certainly got the looks for it.'

Carl still did not hear what Mark was trying to say. For a moment silence hung in the air between them like a cloud uncertain whether to dissolve into rain or disperse.

'Would you like some coffee?' Mark offered.

'Yeah.'

'Black or white?'

'White. I'll come through, help you make it.'

'There's no. . .' Mark's voice died. 'Well, why don't you make it and I'll wash up.'

Mark stood at the sink, more aware of Carl behind him looking through the shelves in search of the coffee jar than

12

of the dishes and cutlery he was perfunctorily splashing water over and wiping. He was as nervous as a teenager on one of his first dates, unsure of himself, of what he should say, of what the other was thinking. For, unlike a bar or a sauna, where there was never any doubt about approaches and rejection, he did not know whether Carl's presence indicated the interest, the availability, the desire that Mark wanted him to feel or merely boredom and the lack of anything else to do.

'Do you like it strong?' Carl's voice shattered his thoughts.

'Not very.' Mark half-turned. 'And milk but no sugar.'

'O.K. Do you know you've got a very cute bum?'

Mark felt his face go deep red as he fumbled for a fork under the suds. 'Do I?'

'Yes, you do.'

'Thanks. I can't comment on yours. I haven't seen it.'

'Maybe you will.'

Was that a come-on or ordinary banter? No longer able to concentrate on the simple tasks of scraping grease and rinsing clean, Mark pushed the remaining dishes to the side, shook the water off his hands and reached for a towel.

'Here,' Carl said. 'Your coffee.'

'Thanks.' He took the mug and was suddenly so aware of Carl, himself and the kitchen round him, of so much information coming in through his senses, that the air felt thick; time seemed to have flowed to a standstill. He wanted to reach out for Carl, to hold him and kiss him, but suspected that to do so would take a year, a generation, and Carl would never wait.

'It's a nice room, this.' Carl spoke and the illusion was gone.

'It's a bit small.' Indeed, if four people ever sat at the table, there would be no room for another to stand by the cooker or work-top. It was, however, bright, and the units were neat and functional and it was pleasant in the morning sun to look out at the trees which hid him from his neighbours. 'Shall we go and sit down again?'

Carl turned and Mark glanced over the loose shirt and

13

baggy jeans. The very shapelessness of the clothes was an attraction, an invitation to imagine the body beneath, the ripples of the spine under the skin, the curve between the buttocks, the pattern of hair on the legs. He had only to make a move. . . As he was about to speak, to make some pointless comment on the television programme they had now forgotten, the frustration and irritation of more aggressive and seldom-evident Mark pushed his hesitation aside and he saw, partly in apprehension, partly in relief, his own hand come up and rest on Carl's shoulder.

There was a pause in which Carl neither spoke nor moved and Mark wondered whether his boldness had lost him his lodger. Then he realised that Carl was waiting, that the boldness appeared no more than timidity, that if he did not make another move quickly, he would certainly lose Carl, if not as a lodger at least as a bed-partner and potential lover.

'Of course,' he said, putting his mug down and placing his other hand round Carl's waist, forcing him to turn back, 'we could always go to bed.' The casual, smooth tone glossed over the beating of his heart and the tension that gripped his stomach and chest.

'Let's do that.' Carl stood a few inches away, his eyes a little below Mark's, his expression both innocent and inviting. It required only the gentlest movement from Mark to lean forward and let his mouth touch Carl's, let his tongue lick at his lips and work its way in.

Two Marks made love. One watched in amusement as they fumbled at each other's clothes, as belts proved difficult to undo, as shoes were kicked off, as underwear was clumsily pushed down legs. He cursed silently as one hand bore the weight of his body and the other tried to wipe excess lubricant onto a towel and cursed again as they searched for a suitable position that was comfortable for both. The other Mark was aware of little more than the curiosity in Carl's eyes, the warmth of his body, the intensity of his love-making, all of which were as potent and liberating as a drug. Carl's presence, his implicit understanding that sex was, or could be, something more

14

than the animal response to the demands of instinct, opened long-closed windows in Mark's mind. It had been weeks since he had had sex – with a loud and distasteful young stockbroker he had met in a disco – and months since the long weekends he had shared with Gene. Life, he suddenly realised, had once again become grey and monotonous, and his emotions had shrunk to the daily contact he had with cynical colleagues and indifferent pupils; Carl, lying silently beside him, hugging him as they fell asleep, reminded him there was so much more.

Not that Carl was another Gene, Mark told himself as they sat together over breakfast. It was not only that Carl was his lodger and might now be wondering whether weekly sessions in Mark's bed were an unwelcome addition to the rent he had to pay, but Carl was a quieter, calmer person, who seemed content to sit munching toast littered with lumps of butter and marmalade and talk about nothing more important than what he and Mark might have to do that day. Gene, in contrast, although a quiet talker and a careful listener, had somehow always given the impression of activity, of being on the point of either going out for a long walk through unknown streets and neighbourhoods or wanting to explain or discuss part of his philosophy, which encompassed everything from his own role as an artist to the spiritual powers he sometimes hinted at, and his often contradictory attitude to Mark in his life. From the very first words they exchanged Mark had been entranced.

They had met in a sauna in Paris, where Mark had gone on the second day of the long weekend he was spending in the city. The same sunshine and heat, which should have persuaded him to seek the shade of some gallery or museum or stretch out in a park, caused the discomfort of sweat and damp clothes which gave him the excuse to search out the baths with a relatively clear conscience. Any guilt he felt did not stem from coming to such a place – indeed it was one of the reasons for his yearly visits – but from the ease with which he gave up his pretensions to culture and the haste with which he surrendered to his sexual drive. Thank God, he told himself, there were no such places in London; he would have plunged into them long ago as eagerly as an addict into an opium den, only to emerge years later, equally gaunt and mindlessly happy.

After an hour of cleansing himself thoroughly in the cold pool and steam room, he was ready to join the other towel-clad bodies that padded through the poorly-lit corridors or loitered by the open cubicles. As usual there were few who attracted him and those soon dwindled to one or two. A youth of about twenty with curly black hair, sharp blue eyes and his towel knotted far below his navel pointedly ignored him to speak to an older man with a hairy body and spreading belly; a young man of about his own age with small nipples on a muscular chest shook his head as Mark hovered by his cubicle; another youth offered only monosyllables in response to Mark's conversation. Such rejections disappointed but did not dishearten, for they were as much a part of the ritual as the sex itself, the first course that aroused the appetite for the meal that was to come; but as time passed and he could not find a partner, the hunger to hold and be held became so persistent as to be almost painful. His discreet glances became open stares, his lack of interest in others uncompromising frowns; the sauna, although small and familiar, became a labyrinth where every figure he was following would turn a corner and disappear while another whose heavy gaze he was trying to avoid seemed to stand at every door and in every corner. At last, tired of wandering, he found an empty cubicle where he could lie on the narrow bed and look out and wait.

Every passer-by looked in, eyes flickering over him in cursory and anonymous inspection. Several returned and leaned briefly against the opposite wall until his scowl drove them away. He was beginning to accept that for once he was unlucky, that he would have to compromise and allow himself to be made love to by someone whose talent lay in his expertise rather than his exterior, when a tall, dark-haired figure with a towel wrapped loosely and modestly around his narrow waist took up the position vacated by half a dozen before. He looked at Mark with

16

neither arrogance nor timidity but an open, searching expression which suggested that the sex he offered would be more than the frantic and selfish friction that the rest would want.

At other times Mark would not hurry to accept the invitation, but he knew he had no choice, that if he did not respond immediately the other would go and he would be left alone for the rest of a wasted evening. So he smiled, and beckoned with a slight movement of his head.

They made love slowly, as if it were an art, not a sport, as if they had known each for years, as if they were each other. Nothing existed for Mark but the body beside him, the dark eyes both curious and tender, the thin but handsome features. The other moaned as Mark's hands and mouth moved over his chest and nipples, down over his stomach, along his thighs and over his groin. Their positions changed and he was kissed so eagerly, so deftly, so carefully, that his body first relaxed, then stirred and finally arched as the pleasure became so intense as to be discomfort. He reached down and pulled the dark hair, the searching eyes, the soft mouth to him, kissing the stranger in gratitude, in desire, kissing as fiercely as if that were his orgasm, as if that were the entry to his being, to his heart.

Afterwards, it seemed to Mark that more had been given than had been expected, that the intimacy had not faded with their hunger, that other emotions waited to be discovered. Afraid to disturb, perhaps destroy, this new and fragile relationship, he lay motionless, his eyes resting on the dim and colourless ceiling. His thoughts were no more than echoes of the love-making that had just ended.

When they at last spoke it was to misunderstand each other's French and to smile as they realised they shared a common tongue. Gene's voice was rich without being deep, rounded with a soft American accent. 'But you look so French,' Mark said, as if apologising for some insult. 'Your hair, your eyes. . .'

'So do you,' Gene told him and Mark found the stare accompanying the remark both pleasing and uncomfortable. Half-expecting Gene to say he was in a hurry, had

17

somewhere to go, Mark suggested they have a drink in the bar and was almost surprised when the American agreed.

They sat facing each other across a low table, apart from the small group at the other end of the room watching the television news. Mark had already learned, as they showered and dried themselves, that Gene came from Chicago, had lived in Paris for a year, was a photographer turning to painting. Now, as they both drank coffee and leaned towards each other as if proximity were a different form of touch, Mark talked about his own ambitions, the kind of songs he tried to write, the tradition that was more French than British or American. Gene listened and asked questions that showed he understood not only Mark's words but the unspoken assumptions, his expression unchanging when Mark confessed that he had no agent, that he had recorded nothing, that his only public performances had been at school concerts and to friends.

It was Mark who proposed they have dinner together, no longer doubting that Gene would accept, but Gene who wanted first to go back, to that room or another, to make love again. There the American lay him down, whispered in his ear, 'This is for you' and with his tongue caressed all of Mark's body, following the flow of his muscles, sucking fingers and toes, exploring the warmth of his armpits and groin. It was not a sexual act but an offering of rest and relaxation as soothing as a massage; tensions which Mark had scarcely been aware of dissolved and he found himself almost crying in relief.

Dark had fallen by the time they left the sauna. With Gene leading the way, they walked through back streets where there was little traffic or movement apart from the occasional pedestrian and the lights from a neighbourhood bar. Mark had considered he knew Paris, but he realised that it was only the superficial knowledge of the visitor who has seen most of the sights, who knows two or three of the Metro lines by heart and who has chosen his favourite cafés by default. These narrow streets and tenements seemed to shelter the real life of the city, from which he was as cut off as if the scene he was

18

passing through was no more than the image projected by an overblown television screen. He envied Gene his familiarity with the city as he envied the fluent French he had overheard and all the other aspects of Gene's character that he had as yet only glimpsed.

They were given a table in the basement of a small Greek restaurant where the subdued lighting and the hubbub and proximity of the other diners offered the same anonymity as would an empty room. They ordered, handed the menus back to the waiter, then Gene turned and smiled and Mark felt as if he were at the brink of a high diving-board, knowing he wanted to dive, knowing that he wanted more than anything the thrill of the plunge, yet not sure he had the courage to make the simple and fatal leap.

'What brought you to Paris?' he asked, the first question that came to him.

'I wanted to get away from America. I'd been here before, when I did Europe as a student and I always wanted to come back. It's the romantic in me, I suppose.' Gene grinned. 'Hemingway, Fitzgerald, Stein; why not me?'

'How did you get a job?'

'I didn't. I was really naive. I went round all the art galleries and photo labs and of course no one wanted an American without a work permit who didn't speak the language very well and who knew nothing about the local scene. I was down to my last hundred francs when I got a job in a bookstore selling pornography.'

'You still do that?'

'From time to time. I get by doing portrait shots and very occasionally pictures for one of the magazines.'

'What about your painting?'

Gene shook his head. 'No money in that yet. I'm still working on it. One day I'll walk into a gallery with one of my pictures and the owner will recognise a masterpiece, and bow and scrape and insist on going back with me there and then to my garret where he'll buy everything for a seven-figure-dollar-sum.'

Mark smiled.

'What about you?' Gene asked. 'Do you come to Paris often?'

'About once a year. Sometimes twice. It's a habit, like going home to see the family.'

'That's another reason I moved here. So I wouldn't have to see mine.'

'Are they so bad?'

'I'll tell you about them sometime.'

Sometime. Was that a promise of the future? Suddenly Mark remembered that time had not stopped, that this togetherness would, later that night or the next morning, come to an end, that two days from now he would be back home, alone, like a beggar brought in for an evening's warmth before being thrown back onto the winter streets. Or did Gene's words suggest more, a challenge to time, a promise that this evening would not end?

'Do you ever go to London?' Mark asked, willing the answer yes.

Gene shook his head. 'I haven't been anywhere. I can't afford it. Don't have the time.'

'You must come.'

'Maybe one day.' The promise faded.

Later in the evening, when they had drunk one bottle of wine and ordered another, when the restaurant was beginning to empty and the sound of others' conversations began to diminish, the routine questions always asked to sketch in another's background had long since given way to a deeper discussion of the kind which Mark seldom had with colleagues and friends. It reminded him that life and its possibilities stretched far beyond the rut of work he found himself in. For Gene talked about what he tried to do with his art, outlined a world where human experience was stripped of words and in images and colour and form rendered somehow richer and more meaningful; and Mark, responding, found himself struggling to understand, to express ideas that had lain for years in his mind, ideas that had frozen into assumptions about his own existence and place in the world. 'But there are limits to our understanding,' he pointed out, 'I can never know what it's like to be someone

20

else – a Frenchwoman, an Indian farmer, a starving African.'

'Can't you?' Gene asked. 'Can't you let go of all your preconceptions, your upbringing – it's just habit anyway – and be, think yourself into being, that person?'

As his arguments and beliefs were gently but firmly swept aside Mark saw in Gene's expression, heard in his voice, the awareness of life that he himself had once had but had lost in the last three years. His vision had narrowed to the texts of Shakespeare and Dickens, Murdoch and Greene, was no broader than that of the teenagers he tried to trick into appreciating them.

'And all I do is teach,' he said.

'What about your songs?'

Mark shrugged. 'I've always kidded myself that teaching was only temporary, that it was only to provide an income till I got somewhere with my music. But it'll never happen. I'm doomed to the classroom for the rest of my life.' He grinned to mask the sudden anguish he felt. It was the first time he had admitted such a possibility – the prospect was a death sentence.

'That's up to you,' Gene said. 'If you've got the talent, go for it. If not, go for it anyway. Plenty of people out there are making fortunes with no talent at all.'

'I know. I just. . .' I just don't see myself that way. But yes, he did. Something about Gene gave Mark confidence, suggested that all he needed was the courage to believe in himself and his talent and he would hear his songs performed all over the world, perhaps even his own voice singing them. 'I just need to work at it, that's all.'

'I'll drink to that,' Gene said, refilling their glasses and raising his own. 'To Mark Whatever-your-last-name-is, singer-songwriter.'

'To Gene From-the-sauna, photographer and highly successful artist.'

'Hey, you are staying with me tonight, aren't you?'

Gene's home was not a garret but a cramped second-floor flat overlooking one of the narrow pedestrian streets in Saint-Michel. 'I sublet from an Argentinian woman,' he explained, calling from the tiny kitchen where he was making coffee. 'I can't use the shower because it leaks into the apartment below and I can't do anything about it in case the landlord finds out I'm here.'

'Where's she?' Mark asked absently as he inspected the photographs and paintings scattered over the walls.

'Leila? Living with her boyfriend – who's a friend of mine, which is how I got the place. She wants this as security in case they ever split up.'

The photographs were portraits, mostly taken in the street, of strangers, Mark presumed, who had caught Gene's attention. They stared into or past the camera with expressions that varied from sadness to humour but always suggesting resilience, an ability to face and overcome obstacles. The few paintings that hung beside them used colour to create warmth and were of groups rather than individuals; one, a soft study of two middle-aged women walking arm-in-arm in a park, particularly appealed to him.

'Are they all yours?' he asked as Gene came in.

'Yes.' Gene smiled in embarrassment. 'Pure egoism, I know.'

'It must be great to live in the centre of town like this.' Mark looked out of the window at the street. Below the darkened or curtained rooms of the buildings opposite some of the restaurants were closing, but the lights of a small supermarket still shone out on the numerous passers-by.

'It has its advantages,' Gene said, coming to stand beside him. 'But I could do with somewhere bigger and with a decent bathroom.' Without warning, he leaned forward and kissed Mark, putting his arms round him so that Mark, had he wanted to, could not get away. He felt for a moment weak, as if he were about to faint, but the awareness of Gene's tongue on his lips brought him back to reality and he hugged Gene, pulling their groins together and slowly rotating his hips.

'I wanted to do that all through dinner,' Gene said when they parted.

'So did I.' To his own ears Mark's response sounded weak.

'When do you have to leave?' Gene asked.

'The day after tomorrow. But I could stay on till Wednesday.'

'Why don't you?'

'No reason.'

'Then do.'

'O.K.' With that word the future was indefinitely postponed, for Wednesday was seventy-two hours away, and in this small room with its mattress on the floor and this handsome American making love as if there were no one else, as if there never could be anyone else to attract him in the world, seventy-two hours was longer than Mark could comprehend, longer than infinity.

The unfamiliar noises of the street woke Mark early and he lay for a time watching Gene sleep, the narrow face half-buried in the pillow, the shoulder gently rising and falling with each breath. Looking round the room, where the morning light was hardly obscured by the thin cloth draped over the window, he saw the easel leaning against a wall and a stack of canvases beside it. He peered at the nearest photograph, a young woman sitting astride a chair, her arms resting on the back, looking at him with an expression of pride or anger, and he suddenly felt depressed. For if Gene came to London, slept with Mark and woke up in his bedroom, all that would greet him would be posters from the Victoria and Albert, stacks of books from university and school and cheap souvenirs collected during various holidays abroad. Nothing, apart from a closed drawer stuffed with music paper and typewritten sheets, gave Mark personality, individuality; nothing at all. Compared to Gene he was hollow, was simply a collection of mannerisms and words bound by routine and habit, apparently three-dimensional but with no more substance than a hologram.

And in a few minutes, an hour at most, Gene would wake, turn to him, greet him, kiss him, perhaps make love, as if Mark were his equal, worthy of his time and respect. If he knew how little there was to Mark, he would surely lose interest, make some excuse to say goodbye and after an awkward breakfast together Mark would find

23

himself walking back to his hotel, wondering whether to spend two more days listlessly wandering through the Louvre and watching the crowds from a café table, or to go home early and try to forget Gene and their conversation and their love-making and what might have been.

Yet last night he had managed to respond on every level, to entertain Gene, to suggest that his music was a talent he was capable of developing. If he was careful, paid attention and did not allow himself to lapse into the kind of unthinking responses he gave his pupils throughout most of a tiring day, he might hang onto the situation, gloss over the emptiness within him and persuade Gene that he was worthy of him. Furthermore, given time, given Gene's presence, he might indeed develop those aspects of his character that had been stifled in the last few years, become what he pretended to be, until the act became second nature and finally his nature itself.

Now, sitting with Carl, facing him over the debris of their breakfast, Mark thought about that second nature. First nurtured and tended by Gene, for months it had been left to struggle on its own. Yet it had not died; stronger than before, it had even rescued him last night, when the old Mark would have sat talking until long after midnight, until they were so tired that they could only go to their separate beds, the opportunity to make love lost under all his procrastinations and doubts. But it was far from reasserting itself completely, Mark knew, for he was uncertain in this new situation, could not imagine how Carl was feeling or how he might react.

'Do you want some more coffee?' he asked, to break the silence.

'No thanks.'

'Toast?'

'No.'

Had he gone too far? Was Carl's friendly but formal tone an indication that last night should not have happened but, since it had, should not be referred to?

'I have to go to the supermarket,' Mark said.

'Now?'

24

'No. Later, sometime. I've got nothing else to do.'

'I thought you said you were going into town.'

Mark shrugged. 'That was just a thought. There's nothing I have to do there.'

'Can I come with you? To the supermarket?'

'Sure. I was intending to show you where it was.'

To give himself something to do, Mark stood up and started clearing the table. Carl sat up, piled plates, swept crumbs into his palm. 'Thanks for breakfast,' he said, staring up at Mark.

Looking down, Mark was aware, as sharply as if he had been kicked, that what he had to do was lean over and kiss Carl, that Carl, far from being upset at what had happened last night, would be more upset if it went no further, if they were to stack dishes by the sink and become once again landlord and lodger. Their lips touched and Carl, as if held by the contact, stood up slowly, gently took the cups and saucers that Mark still held in one hand and placed them on the table. 'I want to go back to bed,' he whispered. 'Will you come?' as if asking for permission, asking for company.

But, a year and a half later, Carl had gone and Ben had arrived and Mark was no more likely to seduce or be seduced by him than he was to flirt with the sour-faced woman who shared his landing. Instead he had Robert, or rather he had had Robert until the previous evening. Now, as he checked the refrigerator and cupboards in the weekly routine of drawing up a shopping list, he thought about the tall figure who was at that moment either waiting to be picked up or already heading north. He would be talking, joking, one of a small group who knew each other intimately, who shared a common interest and goal from which Mark would always be excluded. He wondered what Robert was thinking, whether he had already forgotten last night, pushed it aside to concentrate on the rehearsal and performance or whether it weighed on his mind as heavily as it did on Mark's. And if he was ignoring the others and staring out of the window, his thoughts on Mark, was it in anger or regret, seeing Mark as his lover, with whom he had had no more than a stupid disagreement, or as someone already in his past, someone he had once cared for but who had proved himself too self-centred, too immature?

Arriving at the supermarket earlier than usual, Mark found it more crowded than he was accustomed to. Trying to ignore the women and children who seemed to knock past him or stand in his way intentionally, he made his way slowly up and down the aisles, checking his list and looking out for anything he might have forgotten to write down. Today it was routine, as it had been for many weeks, but it was routine he had once enjoyed and even now he could not come here without thinking of Carl. On that first Saturday they had each collected what they wanted and were both reaching for salt to place in their separate baskets when Mark had pointed out that such a situation was ridiculous, that they should buy together and divide the cost. Carl had gone for a trolley and, offering to cook dinner that night, disappeared down one aisle to reappear at the top of another, his arms full of cans and packets that Mark, with his unimaginative diet, had never considered buying. That had been the first of many weeks when Mark found himself standing by row upon row of biscuits or washing powder, watching Carl darting to and fro or leaning forward to compare prices and contents, a slightly overweight figure with a handsome face and brow furrowed as he looked for something he needed. Mark would realise how happy he was, sharing this mundane chore with someone as attractive, as caring as Carl, his lover. Then what had been irritation dissolved into benevolence as he watched pensioners shuffling from one stand to the next picking up and peering at packets and cans, married couples piling fizzy drinks, kitchen rolls and endless tins of baked beans into their trolleys, and the occasional solitary young man inspecting the shelves as if he were not sure of the system and did not quite understand what he had to do; for whatever these strangers had in their lives, he, Mark, had more. His happiness had reached a peak in December, loading the trolley with bottles of drink, turkey, vegetables, pastry

26

and all the ingredients for the cakes and hors d'oeuvres they later prepared with varying success. It had been as much a celebration as the party they gave, for it was the first Christmas Mark had shared with anyone other than his family; the first Christmas he had been in love, the first, he had thought, of many to come. The memories of later months were duller, sometimes painful, but no less strong, and as he passed one section or another he could hear, as if they for ever gave off the echo, Carl's enthusiasm, his whisper of 'I love you', his anger as they disagreed yet again.

With Gene the supermarket had been different but the emotion had been the same, if not rawer and stronger. The two of them would go down the narrow steep staircase, out and across the street into what was little more than a small, family-run shop where the shelves were so close together and stacked so full that it was difficult for even one person to make his way from one end to the next. Surrounded by the thick aroma of spices, fresh vegetables and fruits, they would study the wide selection of North African produce and pick out packets that they scarcely knew what to do with. Behind the check-out desk there were always two or three Arabs who interrupted their intense conversation to greet Gene in what was to Mark incomprehensible French. By his third or fourth visit they had begun to recognise and welcome him so that he began to feel accepted, to believe that he was putting down roots, that in this minor but important way the world was smiling on his relationship with Gene.

Robert had never come with him to this supermarket. At the weekend, whether at home or with Mark, he would sleep through the morning, only waking slowly and getting up in the early afternoon. At first Mark had resented seeing so many hours wasted, having Robert so close and yet out of reach, had even tried the first or second Saturday to cajole him awake, until he understood how much effort went into a week of classes and rehearsals, of both working for an established company and trying to set up on his own. So, regretting that he was awake and could not join Robert in sleep, Mark would get up, dress, tiptoe out of the room and, after having breakfast and tidying up the kitchen or living-room, set out for the supermarket on his own. Yet because Robert never helped with the housework, only washing dishes or making tea or coffee when prompted, Mark sometimes could not help feeling that despite everything, the long hours they did spend together, the telephone conversations, the meeting again and again and again, Robert was little more than a one-night stand or a friend from out of town who will happily join his host in bed knowing that next day he will be hundreds of miles away. Only when Robert willingly accompanied him here, helped him load a basket or trolley, discussed which was the better buy and what they would cook together for a meal that night would Mark believe in his heart of hearts that their relationship was solid and strong.

It was little after eleven when Mark returned home, put away his purchases and sat down with a cup of coffee to think about the day ahead. Routine dictated that he should dust and vacuum; there was also a cupboard in the hall that had been waiting for weeks to be painted. Knowing Robert was to be away, he had planned a quiet weekend with today spent pottering at household chores and Sunday at the piano, going over some of his early songs and, if his mood was right, writing something new. Now he knew that as long as last night hung over him, until the situation was resolved, he would not be able to settle to anything, even the simple task of clearing out the cupboard and scrubbing down the walls. Besides, the sun that had woken him and whose heat had accompanied him to and from the supermarket still shone and would shine for the rest of the day. To stay in would be at best folly, at worst a punishment; he ought to go somewhere – to Brighton or into the country – but he would not do so alone, and it was now too late to call friends and see if one or another was free. Also the only person he would want to go with was Robert and anyone else's presence would only remind him of Robert's absence.

It was with no certain idea of where he was going or what he intended to do that Mark went out and walked to the underground station. Habit took him in the direction of Hyde Park, a memory of his first months in London when, with nothing to do, he had gone there frequently and walked through it hoping that from among those who passed him or who sat or sprawled on the grass someone would emerge to greet him, invite him to become part of that great sub-culture, the network of lively, intelligent, artistic and mildly rebellious individuals which he was sure was to be found simmering below the silent and disgruntled crowds he saw each morning rush-hour. He had never discovered that underworld and it had slipped from his memory, only returning occasionally when he met someone whose acquaintance suggested that it might indeed exist, but who inevitably disappointed by seeming to lead a life as routine and mundane as Mark's own.

At Oxford Circus, instead of changing to the Central Line, he found himself heading for the exit, his sudden urge to bound up the escalator and stairs impeded by the inevitable tourists debating, no doubt, where they were and what they were about to do. The street was as crowded and he shuffled along the pavement, his impatience giving way to the realisation that he was in no hurry, had nothing to do and it would do no harm if he too were to stop and look at the shop windows he was passing. Perhaps he would see something he could buy for Robert. Meanwhile, at the back of his mind lay the unacknowledged reason for his presence here, his leaving the underground two stops early and joining a crowd, where he always hated to be. For it had been here in Oxford Street, on a Saturday in the early afternoon, that he had first met Robert and this return to that scene was partly to compensate for his absence, to have him somehow nearer, and partly a pilgrimage, a penitence, a prayer that might absolve him of his sin and wash away Robert's resentment.

It had been a little further along, past Bond Street station, that they had first seen each other. It was a spring day, the first suggestion that year of warmth and, while Carl was at work, Mark was idly looking for summer clothes. Attracted by a shirt in its window,

29

he walked into a shop, his eyes crossing with those of a youth pushing open the door. Mark turned, expecting only to see an anonymous back dissolving into the crowds, and almost started at the sight of the tall figure standing by the pavement, at a slight angle to counter the weight of a large bag, staring at him with an expression that registered both expectation and curiosity. Without thinking – for if he had thought he would have blushed, turned away, convinced that the other was waiting for the excuse to be offended, angered, or had mistaken him for someone else – he went over, the world suddenly shrinking to the face he was approaching and his own pounding heart, and said hello.

'Hi.'

'What are you doing?' Mark asked, becoming aware of heavy ear-rings, dark hair surrounding the eyes, a smooth or recently shaved chin, and a loose blue tee-shirt with some colourful design.

'Looking for a birthday present for my mother.' The voice was young, pleasant, with no trace of class or region.

'Here?'

The other smiled, and shifted slightly the position of his bag. 'No. I was just looking around. What about you?'

'I want to buy a shirt. Are you in a hurry? Do you want to come in?'

'Why not?'

Inside, Mark flicked through various stands, seeing only a blur of colour, unable to waste the least concentration on anything other than keeping this youth with him, afraid that he would lose interest and make some excuse to go.

'No, too bright. No. No. I don't like the collar. Not me,' he commented as each shirt passed. 'Oh, forget it, I can't afford it and I don't need one. What about your mother?' he asked, straightening up. 'When's her birthday?'

'Tomorrow.' The other grinned.

'You've left it a bit late. What were you thinking of getting her?'

'I don't know. A scarf, a brooch. I can't afford much.'

'A book?'

'She doesn't read.'

They were back in the street and slowly walking towards Hyde Park. Mark felt as if he were on a tightrope along which he had to move quickly enough to maintain momentum, but not so carelessly that he would lose his balance and fall back into oblivion. He had to keep talking, to portray himself as intelligent and sympathetic, to hold this stranger's attention and prevent him from drifting away, from taking advantage of the first lull in conversation to say goodbye, it's been nice talking to you, and disappear into the crowds. At the same time he could not talk too much and give the impression of over-eagerness, of someone who masked inadequacies in empty phrases and aired prejudices and opinions to whoever would listen.

By the time they reached Selfridges they had exchanged names and Mark had begun to relax, to understand that Robert was as willing as he himself was eager to let their time together continue. Robert had decided to buy perfume and they stood at first one counter then another, examining labels and bottles, spraying and sniffing. With another, Mark might have been embarrassed, but there was nothing effeminate about Robert, no suggestion of campness which might rub onto him. In the end Robert chose, after seeking Mark's approval, a recent blend and, after paying and dropping it into his bag, proposed going to the café for coffee or tea.

'Is that all you have to buy?' Mark asked when they had found a table and made themselves comfortable.

Robert nodded.

'What are you doing afterwards?'

'I have to go home. I'm going out with my family tonight for dinner.'

Mark was aware of a moment's disappointment before he accepted that he could not expect this stranger suddenly to be free, that in Carl his own ties were far stronger and more restricting. 'Anywhere interesting?'

'I don't know. Hampstead, probably.'

They talked about themselves until Mark mentioned he taught English and Robert asked about his favourite period. His own was the sixteenth century with its

31

explosion into life on the stage, and the warmth and depth of early seventeenth-century poetry. Have you read this and that and the other, he asked, and Mark nodded or said he had skimmed through it, or admitted that he had not yet got round to it. Robert did not notice these lapses, and went on to talk about the later classics he was trying to catch up on. Mark listened, charmed, for Robert spoke very differently from his colleagues or the students and lecturers he had known at university, who commented on this book or that author in tones that were outwardly casual but were intended to impress, to make it clear that the speaker kept up with the literary Joneses, could wield such words as contextualisation and sub-plot and talk of influences and subtleties of style with the detached tone of a doctor examining the symptoms of a disease. It was obvious that Robert enjoyed these works for themselves and spoke about them not to impress but to share his enthusiasm, like a man in the desert who discovers a spring and with genuine charity looks for someone to share it with.

'How do you read so much?' Mark asked.

'I read all the time,' Robert said. 'On the tube, on the bus, at home in bed.'

'What do you do?'

'I'm a dancer.'

For a moment the word suggested to Mark discothèques and cabarets. 'You mean ballet?'

'Yes, at the moment. But I'm more interested in modern dance.'

It was not a distinction Mark understood and Robert's explanation only partially clarified it for him. What he did learn was that for Robert dance was a profession, a vocation, not a hobby. 'When I finish two or three seasons where I am now, I want to go abroad and dance with Béjart or Parsons. Then, when I'm ready, I'll start my own company.'

'How old are you?' Mark asked, trying to picture such a career structure.

'Nineteen.'

'Nineteen!' He had thought twenty-four, twenty-five.

'I know I seem in a bit of a rush,' Robert added. 'But dancers have a short life. You're past it by the time you're forty. Anyway, Michael Clarke had his own company when he was twenty-three.'

It wasn't Robert's haste which had astonished Mark but his depth of knowledge, the self-confidence which suggested someone far older and more mature. He was almost as young as the pupils Mark taught, yet apparently shared none of their preoccupations, their contempt for what did not immediately interest them, their need to assert themselves and claim an identity through extremes of dress and behaviour. Mark was fascinated, captivated, had not felt so attracted and excited by an individual since Gene two years before. Then he had been younger, inexperienced, had been at times overawed by the American, but with Robert he felt no such inferiority, was sure they were on an equal plane.

From dance they moved on to Mark's music, to the demonstration tape he would shortly make, the studio where he was going to record. In the summer, he said, I won't take a holiday. I'll spend days chasing up agents and record companies and getting myself bookings. I'll annoy people so much they'll listen to me, give me an audition just to shut me up. And if I can't get the right musical backing I'll go solo. The songs are strong enough; all I need is to project myself more. In the past he had spoken this way as much to convince himself as the person he was with, but today he knew it was all true, that it was not another vague project which could be conveniently abandoned when a minor difficulty stood in its way but a resolve, a decision which could no longer be reversed.

As they continued to talk, Mark's awareness of Robert's physical attractiveness, which, at the moment of their meeting had caused him to turn in a reaction more reflex than voluntary, but had since demanded no more of his thoughts than the presence of a person sitting silent in the same room, came once again to the fore. It was not mere sexual desire – indeed there was a blank in his imagination where he would otherwise have a clear picture of who would do what to whom – but rather a curiosity, a wish to kiss Robert, to put his arms round him and see where those actions would lead. Their embrace, his hands moulding Robert's shoulders, his back, his waist, would be as much an exploration of Robert's personality, his thoughts and emotions as their conversation had been. To go further, to undress, to let their hands cautiously pass the barriers of belt and zip and their mouths stray down to nipples and chest, would be as momentous, as awesome as searching for and finding each other's soul.

But nothing that Robert had said or done had suggested he would welcome such intimacy. If they had spoken in a gay pub or disco the question would have been irrelevant, but meeting in the street let in the doubt that Robert was one of those rare individuals who speak to strangers merely to pass the time or in the hope of making a new friend. If they were both gay, to reassure each other they should have mentioned clubs they knew, bars they drank in – a minor but significant ritual as necessary, and almost as melodramatic, as the passwords of spies and the secret handshakes of cabals. But the conversation had not moved in that direction and Mark, while wanting to confirm that Robert was gay, could not crassly interrupt its flow and send it in a quite different direction. Besides, there was a piquancy in the uncertainty, in the possibility that Robert's interest in Mark was no more than the curiosity of youth, a desire to meet everyone and learn everything. In which case they could talk and talk and not only would Mark's time be enjoyably spent, but he would able to return to Carl with an unwillingly clear conscience. To bring the subject into the open, as well as complicating matters for himself, might only make Robert feel uneasy, obliged to repel advances that had not been sought and to bring the afternoon to a swift and unpleasant end.

There was a moment of silence. Robert was sitting back, his legs splayed out under the table on either side of Mark's. Mark leaned against the wall, watching the sachet of sugar that his right hand was turning over and over. In a moment they would start talking again, start following paths which, having skirted their outer shells, would probe gradually deeper and Mark would find the attraction stronger, the desire to go on and on much more difficult to resist. It was with as much relief as regret, therefore, that he saw Robert look at his watch and announce he had to go and with unexpected elation that he heard Robert say, 'Can we meet again? Tomorrow?'

I don't know, he had said, promising to phone, but not giving his own number. They had parted in the street and Mark had watched Robert run for a bus before turning away and walking towards Hyde Park as he was doing today. He wondered how much of that first meeting Robert remembered, whether every detail was clear or if it was no more than a haze in which only a word, a gesture, an expression in Mark's eyes could be distinguished. Wherever he was now, in whichever community hall or small theatre the company had ended up, he was certainly not thinking of Mark. Mark knew, from having seen Robert rehearse and perform, that once on the floor, in costume or his old leotard, surrounded by the other dancers and listening only to the music and the choreographer's instructions, nothing existed for him except his own body and the role it had to play. 'It's as if I were in clothes that were a little too big for me,' he had once explained, 'and somehow I had to make myself bigger so that I could fit into them. It requires all my concentration, but I know, I know,' he emphasised, 'I can do it.' Mark had watched, envious of the ability and confidence that allowed Robert to dive into, become his art, as he now knew that Robert would have forgotten him, would be no more than the worker or the clown of whichever dance was being rehearsed, while Mark wandered about London, obsessed by a problem he had created and could not resolve.

The few men on soap-boxes at Speakers' Corner surrounded by small crowds did not tempt Mark, as they had done years before, to stop, listen and sometimes interrupt when the argument strayed beyond elementary logic. Walking on towards the Serpentine, he slowed his natural, impatient pace to that of the many around him.

The park was studded with the middle-aged and old in deckchairs, and the young, shirtless, in shorts, stretched out on the grass or played football, threw frisbees or ran with their dogs. One woman, as if triggered by his passing, suddenly stood up and energetically waved her arms as she stared into the distance: 'Bill! Over here! We're here, Bill!' Mark stared in the direction she was facing and could see no response from the figures approaching. Maybe, he thought, it is not a particular Bill she wants, but anyone of that name; maybe he is needed to fulfil some magic ritual. There is a certain ghastly, evil spell which can only be performed in Hyde Park on a sunny day and needs the sacrifice of an unknown man named Bill. . .

He passed a couple kissing and in envious anger looked away. This park is not big enough; people should not be able to find each other. Or if they do, it should be by chance, by miracle. Imagine planning to meet someone here and forgetting to specify exactly where. Someone you can't contact in any other way. . . You can't find him and so you go home and come back the next day at the same time and the day after that and so on and so on. Or there is someone you can only meet in the park; someone who has a husband, a lover elsewhere, whom he or she can never leave and you understand and you're not jealous, just never fulfilled . . . 'the path that winds for ever through the trees', 'late again, rain again, time to go home', 'and still I cannot see what can ever set me free.' The phrases presented themselves like actors for an audition uncertain what kind of play the director proposes. There was a song there, Mark knew, and his attention withdrew to play with ideas, to hum different notes, to draw words at random and see what emotions they evoked. A song about sadness, with the park, the path, symbolising solitude, the future, whatever. . .

He had walked along the Serpentine with Robert on that second day. Knowing his time was limited, that he had to meet Carl when the pub closed, he had phoned Robert to tell him he could spare an hour, the guilt which had tried to prevent him from making the call drowned

36

out by his excitement. They talked less seriously than on the previous day and discovered a strong sense of humour in common, an ability to see the ridiculous almost everywhere they looked. Their backgrounds were sketched in further; Mark learning that Robert's parents were divorced, that he lived with his mother and elder sister. 'I'm the black sheep,' he said. 'Everyone else is very money-conscious, very ordinary.' Mark spoke about his own parents and brothers, the ties that had never been strong and which had frayed to no more than the occasional telephone call and the last-minute decision as to whether to visit at Christmas. And still neither spoke about being gay, although Mark had slipped the word in when talking about his songs and had mentioned the person he lived with was male. If he continued to avoid the subject, it was as much a reaction to the long conversations of his younger days when it had seemed important to go into every detail of his own and others' sexuality, to talk about backgrounds and coming out and first love affairs. Now, even if Robert were not offended, crudely to ask whether he was gay, to say he wanted to go to bed with him, would be naivety, would destroy any image of himself as adult and mature.

When they separated at Knightsbridge, Mark had to restrain himself from hugging Robert, from embracing the tall, strong body that had begun to imprint itself on his memory, from kissing the wide mouth which hinted knowledge, a certain weariness with the world. But when Robert asked if they could meet on Tuesday evening, suggested Leicester Square at eight o'clock, Mark's conscience unexpectedly made itself heard. 'I might not be able to make it.' 'Try,' Robert said and for that one word, for the near-pleading in his eyes, Mark knew that even if it meant lying to Carl, he would be there, early, waiting, as impatient and nervous as he always had been at the start of a love affair.

Parks were also associated with Gene; on their first day together they had gone to the Bois de Boulogne and walked there for hours. When Gene had eventually woken that first morning, it had been to make love again wordlessly and the act, slow, sleepy, had drained Mark's fears, instilled a rare confidence, allowed him to laugh away the idea that Gene might lose interest, might find him lacking some essential trait. After dressing, they had gone out to the supermarket and disagreed only on who should pay for the various purchases. These, although no more than butter, coffee, bread and jam, were made exotic by their wrappings, and the French that Mark could easily understand but which nevertheless appeared to be more than mere instructions or ingredients. After breakfast they had washed in the kitchen, a clumsy process interrupted by Gene holding and kissing Mark, actions that were less expressive of sex than of affection. For Mark it was a novelty to find someone who continued to be physically attracted to him rather than suggesting he was outstaying his welcome. On other mornings those who Mark longed to have stay soon made excuses and left, seldom to be seen again while those who lingered over breakfast revealed themselves as bigots or bores and their attempts at caresses as obsessive pawing. Each kiss of Gene's, however, each time his hand held Mark's waist or rubbed a damp cloth down his back or between his legs, was physical proof of an emotion that was growing as fast as the others had diminished.

They walked across the Seine and the Ile de la Cité to take the metro at Châtelet. The wide passageways with the long tall posters, the rumbling of the trains and the pungent smell of burning oil were both familiar and new, as if each time in the past that he had taken the Paris underground it had been a foretaste, a reassurance that one day he would meet Gene. Now he stood, hanging onto the strap, gently pulled from side to side, facing this gaunt American who smiled at him and he knew that all the stories, all the books he had read about falling in love, about the intensity of the experience, were finally coming true.

'I love coming here,' Gene said once they were among the trees and walking away from the main road. 'It reminds me a little of home.'

'Does Chicago have somewhere like this?'

'Not Chicago. Wisconsin, Michigan, the woods there. I used to go camping with my father when I was ten, eleven, twelve. He went for the hunting and I came along just to get away from the city. We argued a lot. Not so much because he was killing animals, but because of the noise his gun made. Everything would be so peaceful and quiet, just the birds and the trees swaying in the wind. I loved it like that. But suddenly there'd be an explosion because Dad had seen a rabbit or a duck and shot at it. He usually missed it.'

'I've never been hunting. My father never took us anywhere. He expected us to look after ourselves. I think he saw my brothers and me as a kind of burden he couldn't avoid, like taxes.'

'I'd like to live out in the country. Maybe in the Alps or up in the Rockies, an eccentric artist – and his lover – gradually growing old.'

They walked on, came to a road, crossed it and were again surrounded by trees.

'Tell me more about the eccentric artist,' Mark asked.

'What do you want to know?'

'What makes you eccentric?'

'Aren't all the best artists eccentric?'

'I don't know. I've never met one.'

Gene did not seem to want to go on.

'You seem very ordinary to me. No, that's not true,' Mark contradicted himself. 'You seem very lucky, able to do what you want to do, and very happy.'

'I am happy,' Gene said, momentarily turning and catching Mark's eyes.

'Because. . .?' Because of me? But the question would have been more than presumptuous; it would have been stupid.

'Because. . . because I believe I understand why I'm here, who I am, what I do.'

Mark waited for Gene to say more and when he did not, prompted, 'Go on.'

'That's all.'

'Why are you here?'

'To paint. To show others what I see, to teach them in some way, to help them understand.'

'Understand what?'

'Understand themselves, understand each other. *Comprendre tout, c'est pardonner tout.*'

'Are we all here for a reason?' Mark asked, wondering where the conversation was taking them, wondering whether to be fascinated, bored or alarmed.

'Of course.'

'What's my reason?'

'To be a singer, to be a teacher. I don't know. I don't know you well enough.'

'Who put us here?' Mark asked, interested in Gene's answer but also aware that he was slipping back into his university days, when he would debate any point to flex his powers of argument like a young animal testing its strength.

'I don't know.'

'Some god?'

'Maybe. It's not important. I'm not ready yet. I'll find out later, if at all.'

'But what good does it do you?'

'What?'

'This . . . this belief that we're here for a reason?'

'It gives me confidence. It lets me relax.' Gene shrugged his shoulders as if the answer were not important.

There was a pause. A middle-aged couple were approaching, she talking, he listening attentively. The man wore a beret and that, with the rapid French he overheard and did not understand, reminded Mark he was in a foreign country, where perhaps nothing was totally familiar.

'I'm crazy,' Gene said when the two had passed.

'I don't think so,' Mark told him. 'And if you are, I envy you your craziness.'

Gene would not be prompted again. 'Tell me about your school.'

'It's big, it's old, it's in the suburbs;' – Dulwich – 'there's nothing special about it.' Mark tried to imagine what American schools were like to make a comparison. 'It's not very violent – we're in the wrong part of town. It's not very mixed either – a few Asians, very few West Indians.'

'Do you get paid well?'

'We get paid. Some people would say that was enough. Ever since I started there have been strikes or threats of strikes and industrial action and God knows what. There was one year I seemed to be out of the classroom more often than I was in it.'

'But you got the rise you wanted?'

'I don't know. I don't care. I try not to think of myself as a teacher. I want to get out. I want to sing.'

'Why don't you?'

It was a question Mark had asked himself and answered many times before, but he wanted to think again before replying to Gene. 'Because I don't have confidence in myself. If I quit this job and then fail as a singer, I couldn't go back into teaching. Not because there are no jobs, but because I would have lost interest, lost the rhythm.'

'Sing something to me.'

'Now? Not without a piano.'

'Well, tell me about your songs. What are they about?'

'A lot of them are about love. Some are what you might call protest songs, but not so direct. One or two I can't define – they're like abstract paintings.'

'And the music?'

'That's the weak bit. It's too derivative. Bits of American folk and British pop and Moustaki and Brel and Lenorman. I never had any formal training.'

'Why not?'

'Because. . .' Again Mark needed to think, to make sure that the answer he gave was the reality and not an excuse, even if the excuse was part of the reality. 'I'd been playing the piano since I was about seven or eight. I played the flute in the school orchestra and the music teacher wanted me to follow music as a career – he was a shy old man everyone seemed to ignore and it would have made him really happy if one of his students had gone to the Royal College of Music and ended up in the Royal Philharmonic or at Covent Garden. But I wasn't interested and probably wasn't good enough. At that time musicians to me were

41

either snobs who wore bow ties and played nothing but the classics or punks who thought that by screaming loudly enough they could bring down the whole of British civilisation – or whatever's left of it. I didn't see myself as either. I was good at English and History and I thought the safest thing to do was go to university and see what happened there.'

'Go on,' Gene said when Mark stopped.

'That's all.'

'So what are you doing now to become a singer?'

'Nothing, to be honest. Or very little. I don't know if I'm good enough. I can't hear myself sing. Sometimes I wonder if all my songs aren't the same – the music's repetitive, the rhymes are too obvious and there's nothing new in my words.'

'You could say the same of Frank Sinatra.'

'I don't want to be a Frank Sinatra.'

'You won't be anyone if you don't try.'

The tone was gentle, inoffensive, and as painful as a blow. Not because it threatened anonymity or Mark's success as a singer, but because it implied, so Mark inferred, that if he were no more than a teacher, one of thousands, millions, who had their mortgage, daily routine and annual holiday abroad, Gene would lose interest in him. One more step, one more admission of inability, of lack of talent, and Mark would have stumbled over the abyss; what he had feared that morning as Gene slept beside him would come true and he would find himself once again alone.

'You're right,' he said. 'I'm just being negative. Let's talk about something else.'

Gene shrugged and Mark was tempted to go on and say believe me, it's true, I really am a great musician, I've got a great voice, I just need the breaks, no, I haven't got round to making the breaks, but I'm working on it; but he kept silent, knowing that anything more he said would be to protest too much, would further convince Gene not of his talent but of his mediocrity.

'Do you want to get your things from the hotel this afternoon?' Gene asked. 'Bring them over to my place?

Hey,' he went on, 'if we don't get there soon, they'll charge you for tonight as well.'

As Gene's last words had stung so these were balm. His worry forgotten, he wanted to kiss Gene, to hug him, to knock him over with joy and affection. 'You're sure you want me?' he teased, putting an arm round Gene's shoulder.

'Sure I'm sure.'

'O.K.,' Mark said and kissed him as they continued walking, so that they stumbled and almost fell, and holding onto each other they burst out laughing.

That first weekend he had laughed a lot with Gene. With Robert he laughed even more. Carl had a sense of humour too, but it was usually sparked by other things, seldom by the two of them together.

Robert's natural expression was demanding, Gene's relaxed but curious, Carl's defiant.

Gene waiting at the airport, at ease, patient.

Carl giving him a birthday present, worried that it might not please.

Robert on stage searching for him in the audience, smiling broadly as their eyes met.

Mark coming home from school and Carl bringing him tea and telling him what he was making for dinner.

Gene talking to him and reassuring him and showing him what he could yet be.

Robert making jokes and discussing art and literature, buying him small presents and forgetting to phone.

Carl's pride, Gene's distance, Robert's resolve.

Making love with Gene in the sauna and on the floor, with Carl on the sofa and in front of the fire, with Robert in bed as the rain poured down.

Out of breath, over the phone, telling Robert he loved him. Never telling Gene he loved him. And Carl. . .

The room's only light came from the orange of the gas fire and the flickering colours of the silent television. Mark lay on the couch, his back aching slightly where it had rested against the rigid arm, and looked at Carl's face, where the lines of beauty were shadowed like an actor made up as an old man. They were silent, allowing the growing intimacy of the day they had just spent to flourish and blossom in the warmth of the late autumn evening. Mark was conscious of the privilege that on a Saturday, the busiest night of the week, Carl had taken time off, put his job at risk, simply to stay in and be with him. Yet in a sense it had been inevitable for they had woken late, had breakfast at noon, gone shopping and arrived back in the late afternoon feeling that the day had only just begun. For Carl to have gone into work as if it were any other night, to have spent hours serving drinks, clearing and washing glasses, calculating, straining to hear orders above the beat of disco, laughing, talking, arguing, would have been to lose, perhaps indefinitely, the rhythm they had found with each other, the new awareness, the stronger affection. So Carl had telephoned, said he was ill while making no effort to sound so, confidence in his skills as a bartender allowing him to shrug off the suggestion that for one night's absence he might be fired. It was Mark who heard the whisperings of guilt, who fully appreciated what Carl had done, who thought of the money unearned. Carl, conscience untroubled, had prepared a generous dinner while Mark had watched and poured wine and washed utensil after utensil. Now, the meal over and the plates piled forgotten in the sink, they sat relaxed, watching each other, waiting.

'Go on,' Mark said, breaking the silence. 'Tell me more.'

'About Edwin?'

Mark nodded. It no longer worried him to hear about this lover, this distant rival. Carl had mentioned before, soon after they first slept together, that there was someone he might return to when London lost its appeal. The subject had come up again this evening as each had opened up his past, Carl explaining that Edwin was in a relationship he did not like, that he was waiting for the right moment to leave, that they had talked about opening a hotel together, a bar or night-club in some small Northern town. Mark listened, needing not only

44

to hear more, to understand better Carl's background and personality, but also to prove to Carl that he could be generous, that he could accept that Carl had other emotional commitments, that jealousy was not part of his make-up. He felt in control of the situation and that control was liberating, a source of strength and pride.

Carl shrugged, not sure what to say.

'When are you going to see him again?' Mark asked.

'I don't know. When I go home for Christmas, I expect.'

'Will you spend it with him or your family?' Or with me?

'I may stay here.'

Another step forward. Mark's expression, shifting from curiosity into sympathy, hid a surge of emotion, a growing sense that he knew exactly what Carl was thinking, that he could predict each word Carl was about to say.

'I. . .' Carl began. Their eyes held. For all the evening's intimacy, for all the pleasure he obviously took in Mark's company, Carl looked unhappy and confused. 'I don't know what to do.'

'I don't understand,' Mark said, although he did, clearly.

'You mean so much to me.'

When younger, with others, even a few months before, with Gene, Mark would have rushed to whoever spoke these words, kissed him again and again, made wild declarations of love and devotion in gratitude for what he had just heard. Now he did not move, determined, before he committed himself, to draw from Carl every drop of emotion, every word of confession that he could. 'You mean a lot to me too.' That was so much an understatement it was almost untrue; for the last two months every moment his attention was not taken by teaching, disciplining or correcting he had been aware of Carl, whether they were together eating, watching television, shopping or making love, or separated by having to leave the flat each morning and sit in the tube without him, by waiting each evening at home, trying to imagine Carl at work.

'Do I?' Carl's eyes clung to Mark as miserably as those of a child in fear of being sent away.

'A hell of a lot.'

The room, its half-light and stuffy warmth, had become all Mark's emotions, with Carl its focus and his heart.

'I love you.' Tears streamed down Carl's face as uninhibited as the joy and pride exploding within Mark. For the first time someone unprompted had told him he loved him; someone had seen him as worthy to love, someone whose word could be trusted, someone whose feelings were as strong as his own. He watched Carl for a second, rejoicing in his triumph, before pity took over and he went to sit on Carl's lap, to stare at him, to see him afresh, to wipe his cheeks dry. 'I love you,' Carl repeated.

'I love you too,' Mark said and leaned forward to kiss him gently, reassuringly and chastely on the mouth. As he did so he realised that what he had said was true, that his pity had been a momentary arrogance of which he should have been ashamed, that his deepest feeling for Carl was indeed love, a desire to be with him always, to protect and be protected by him, to be worthy of him.

'I didn't know if you did.' The tears had stopped but the red eyes and searching look showed that the unhappiness and uncertainty still remained.

'Fool.' Mark smiled. 'Why do you think you're still here?'

'I don't know, I. . .'

'Because I love you. I love you. Despite the fact you have knobbly knees that are painful to sit on and are probably leaving a permanent indentation in my backside.'

Carl grinned and the intensity of the last few minutes melted into an easy comfort. I do love him, Mark told himself. Not just because he's blond and handsome and does all my cooking for me and not just because he tells me he loves me, but because he is wonderful, because he's kind and loves me for what I am rather than for what I want to be, and he *is* a great cook and he makes me happy and. . .

He leaned forward and pulled Carl to him, not to kiss but to hold. Then, because that was uncomfortable, he slid off Carl's knees onto the rug in front of the fire, pulling Carl down with him. They stretched out, holding each other, stroking each other's hair, saying nothing, letting their eyes flicker over each other and express all the emotions they could not put into words. I love him, Mark thought, and wondered why he could not say it again. Instead, he leaned forward and kissed Carl as tenderly, as lovingly, as sexlessly as he could. Carl, however, responded more carnally and soon, although their movements remained slow and unhurried, it was clear what both of them wanted to do. Why not, thought Mark; this time they really would be making love.

Even at the very end they still made love, sometimes able to overcome the anger that had come between them, transform it, if not into affection, then at least into the recognition that they were a couple, that they belonged together. That feeling of warmth, of closeness, had died when Carl left and had never been quite replaced by Robert.

He had followed the Serpentine, crossed over into Kensington Gardens and was now following a path that would take him to Bayswater Road. From there he would walk to Notting Hill Gate and the pub he had often gone to when he first arrived in London but had not visited for over a year. With Carl it had been second nature to have a drink in a gay bar any time they were out together, but Robert avoided them, said he found the atmosphere unpleasant, oppressive and cloying. Mark, remembering darkened rooms surrounded by anonymous and unattractive figures, agreed, unwilling to confess to the hours he had spent watching, waiting, drinking but never getting drunk, hoping but never expecting – and seldom acting to realise his hope – that someone would look out of the crowd, suddenly spotlit as on a stage, those surrounding him fading into darkness, to recognise and be recognised by Mark as the one, the only true lover. It had never happened, would never happen; love could not be arranged, was dependent on coincidence, on two people crossing in a clothing shop door, on an advertisement for a lodger catching an individual's eye, on visiting a sauna because a shower leaked.

He pushed open the door and walked into a room where only the shape conformed to his memory. The pastel colours of recent redecoration and the sunlight flooding in through the wide windows suggested that the crowd of people standing alone or grouped in conversation and laughter were ordinary people having an early afternoon drink rather than individuals whose past activities and present intentions were matters they preferred to reveal only in the murky light of gay bars. Relieved that instead of stepping back into his past he had merely stepped into a pub, he joined those waiting to be served and, once his drink was in his hand, turned to look at those around him.

There were two or three faces he recognised, people he had spoken to years before, whose names he had once known and whose houses he had occasionally visited. Now their eyes passed blankly over him as if he was only one more stranger, another undistinguished face. Whether their lack of recognition was feigned or real Mark did not care; at the time he had enjoyed their company and been pleased to know that he could find someone to talk to but now he realised that they had never offered more than cynical humour and disguised prejudice, that his youth and ignorance had endowed them with a wit and intelligence they did not possess. Furthermore, the fact that they were still here, older, more worn, their hair thinning or greying, that they came back, made the same conversation, cracked the same jokes (or so it seemed from their expressions), suggested that their lives were the same, that they had been nowhere and done nothing, that they were, in short, failures who would be coming here until they died, becoming ever more rigid and disillusioned, laying down their little laws and precepts to whoever in each year's crop of young men cared to listen.

Other faces were familiar from other bars. Mark smiled at one who raised his glass to him, but he had no wish to go over, to join in a perfunctory conversation where each would strain to remember what the other did, where he lived, whether he had a lover, in order to be able to ask the superficial questions that passed for interest in the other's life. The only person Mark wanted to speak to was Robert and he was all but inaccessible. Staring for a moment at the public telephone Mark considered ringing the operator, trying to describe the theatre, hoping he or she would be able to work out its name and locate its number, then dialling, speaking to some old caretaker who would grumble that the dancers were at the other end of the building and he thought they had gone to lunch anyway, persuading him to go over and interrupt a particularly difficult movement and have Robert come to the phone. And even if he had enough coins to keep the line open, to wait until Robert, confused, irritated, worried, picked up the receiver, what would he say? I just wanted to say hello, I miss you, how's it going, tell me everything's all right. The result of which would be to make Robert really angry, to convince him that Mark was weak, uncertain of himself, immature, to complete the break that had been threatened the night before.

He pushed Robert into the background and made himself become once again aware of those around him, searching out from force of habit rather than conscious desire those who attracted him. There were two or three whose good looks implied humour, intelligence, or their own way of looking at the world but, thank God, his solitude did not oblige him to stand and watch them, to try to express all the virtues of his personality in the curve of his smile or the wrinkles of his brow. It was not them but an older face, half-shielded by another, that seized his attention and he looked again, waiting until it came fully into view. The obtrusive figure moved and Mark saw the thin, tired features of someone he had once known. Unwilling to stare, to renew what might be an embarrassing acquaintance, he turned away and tried to remember when and how they had known each other. It was not here – the face was much deeper in Mark's memory. It was years ago Mark now recalled, when he was a student, during his first term and his first months in the city.

He had heard about other students who sowed every imaginable wild oat as soon as they left home, who alternated nights of alcohol and drugs with days of hangover and withdrawal, who slept with someone different each night or immersed themselves in political activity of one or other esoteric extreme. Whether their exploits were real or exaggerated, Mark envied them, wished he too could throw himself overboard and regretted that the fear of consequences – an overdrawn bank account, physical pain, the possibility of arrest, failed exams – held him back. To a certain extent, however, his life had changed; after spending the last year making occasional furtive visits to his home town's only gay bar, he now went out almost every night to the many London had to offer. His initial expectation that each would be different, would specialise in a different type, whether students like himself, drag queens, men in leather, old-age pensioners or any other common factor he could imagine, was soon proved false, and he understood that there was no one pub or club where every customer came close to his ideal, where disappointment with one would be quickly replaced by success with the next. Nonetheless he still hoped each time he went out that tonight would be the night when he would meet the young man he longed for, the one who would prove to him that being gay meant more than clumsy gropings at the end of an evening with someone who was tired, half-drunk and taking advantage of his wife's or lover's absence.

It was on a Saturday night in a pub south of the river where Mark stood with his back to those intent on drinking, facing the small dance floor and watching those on and around it, that he was approached and asked if he wanted to dance. In the gloom he saw someone of his own age and height, with a face that was confident but kind and speaking in the London accent which still sounded to him exotic. He nodded and found himself moving to the music, the alcohol he had taken being enough to overcome his reticence and give him energy and style. His partner moved well and, unlike the others whose eyes glazed over and slipped from ceiling to floor or light to darkness like a man trying to stay upright on a sea of ice, kept watching Mark, paying him an attention that was both flattering and exciting. Mark in his turn stared at him, trying to deduce his character from his appearance, but all he saw was an open-necked shirt and black trousers and jacket, a jaw that was neither round nor square, and untidy hair. It did not matter; it was enough to know someone attractive, his own age, was attracted to him.

They had danced for a quarter of an hour when the other took advantage of a change in the rhythm to shout in Mark's ear, 'Shall we go?' At another time he would have hesitated, wanted to drink and talk first, to learn more about this stranger, but tonight he was impatient, said yes immediately and they turned and left the floor.

'I live quite near,' his new companion said, not so much in invitation as commenting they would not have far to go. 'What's your name?' he asked as they set off.

'Mark.'

'Mine's Tony.'

They were momentarily silent as they crossed the street.

'Do you go there often?' Tony went on.

'My first time. What about you?'

'I go there all the time.' He grinned as if it were a bad habit he ought to give up. 'What do you do?'

'I'm a student. At London University. English.'

Mark expected some comment but there was none. 'What do you do?' he asked.

'Nothing. I've been made redundant. There was an accident at work.'

As if he had been told that famine not only existed but there was a starving African family across the street, Mark stared at Tony. They were passing into the light of a street lamp and he saw with a disappointment that left an echo rather than lingered that Tony was much older than he had thought, was in his mid or even late twenties, that there was a tiredness about his expression that he had not noticed.

'What happened?'

'My ear-drum got punctured.'

'Recently?'

In the short time it took them to reach Tony's front door Mark learned that he had been a chef in a large hotel,

51

that he had tripped on a cloth that someone had left on the floor and had fallen against a spike of some sort on the wall, that he was now suing the management. The unfamiliarity of the situation gave it an air of mellow unreality which overlay the details of ambulances and redundancy and more than compensated for the discovery that Tony's age and experience made him almost of a different generation from himself.

The hall was bare, grey paint flaking and a carpet whose pattern was faded with age and dirt; it announced as clearly as the battery of bells outside that this was a house of bedsits, of anonymity and transience. Tony's was the first door they came to. The room it revealed was large, unequally divided by open shelves, with a wash-basin and tiny cooker on one side and an open wardrobe, an old chair and a mattress piled high with unmade bedclothes covering most of the floor that was left. Weak light came from an orange bulb and there was a strong but not unpleasant smell of soap and humanity.

'It isn't much but it's home,' Tony said.

'I like it,' said Mark. He was not lying; the room was somehow more real than either the clean, conventionally decorated house that his parents owned or the institutional hall of residence he now lived in.

'You want some beer?' Tony asked, opening a tiny fridge under the gas rings.

'No thanks.'

Tony took out a can, pulled off the ring. Mark stood, wondering whether to sit down.

'Hey,' Tony said, not drinking but putting his arms round Mark, 'I'm glad you're here.'

They made love in the dark with only the light from the stereo console, the blankets giving way and collapsing over them like the waves of the sea, their coarseness both warm and reassuring. The record that was playing was vaguely familiar, a deep, obsessively repetitive piece that built up to a crescendo that Mark so hated to hear end that Tony, perhaps understanding that the music was as important an element of their sex as his own body and presence, played it again and again.

52

Mark had always felt clumsy, felt, each time he kissed or held his partner, tried to induce the other's orgasm with his mouth rather than his hands, that the action had been mechanical, skill-less, bringing him little pleasure and the other no more than release. With Tony, however, the awkwardness and fumbling melted into flowing movements where his hands and body and mouth always seemed to be in the right position, to be doing the right things. The credit was Tony's, he knew – he was only responding to what Tony initiated – but nevertheless he felt himself to be an equal partner, to be giving in his own way as much pleasure as he was receiving. And, unlike before, it seemed to go on for ever; the only measurement of time was the pause when Tony, his body covering Mark's to keep him warm, to keep him close, reached over and repositioned the needle on the record yet another time.

When Mark, his head back on the pillow, his eyes barely open, was aware of Tony sitting up, reaching over for a bottle from which he poured a liquid that he began massaging along the curve between Mark's buttocks, he was momentarily alarmed, remembering other rooms, other people, and their rough and impatient attempts to force themselves into him. Then he had either refused or, for reasons of politeness or guilt that he might have inadvertently made an offer that had been misunderstood, had given in and suffered an act which was more uncomfortable than painful, and which only dimly reflected the pleasure that others proclaimed. Tony's hands were so gentle, however, one relaxing, reassuring, wooing him, a finger probing, occasionally tentatively entering, the other more aggressively stroking and grasping his erection, that Mark soon found he wanted the sensation to be both stronger and deeper, that there was an emptiness inside him that longed to be filled and he raised his hips and pushed them against Tony in mute request.

There was a hiatus like a car changing gear, a speaker taking breath, as Tony smeared himself with the oil and gently raised Mark's legs. Where he expected to feel pain there was only the slight pressure of a hand at the mouth of a glove. 'Relax,' he heard. 'Push against me,' and then he was aware of his body drawing Tony in, enclosing him, enfolding him and through the mists of his thought it occurred to him with mild surprise that this action was giving Tony as much as he himself was receiving, that he was not merely an object, a body that Tony was using, but a bringer of different but equally valuable gifts.

When he felt the hardness of Tony's pelvis against his own and his body accept Tony within him as if that was how it should always be, he wanted only to lie there, to drift into a state that was as pleasant as sleep but more intense, from which he would awake not only refreshed but renewed, a butterfly emerged from its chrysalis, a meditator released into a higher state of consciousness. But Tony began to retract and, before Mark could protest, to slide back in, repeating the action again and again. The moment of clarity passed; the sensation thickened and spread from his bowels to the rest of his body, tightening his chest, opening his mouth and drying his throat. He recognised it as the approach of orgasm, but one deeper, more muffled, more threatening than he had ever had before. In reflex he put his hand on his erection and started rubbing frantically before the words 'Don't come! Don't come!' made themselves understood and he slowed the pace. He was aware that his body was being almost violently rocked, that the muscles in his legs were beginning to tire, that his back was pressed against something hard and uncomfortable, but these sensations drowned under the waves that were flooding, exploding from his centre, so strong that he feared he would come apart or pass out. Above him he could hear faster and faster breathing, panting, groaning, words that were both exultation and warning and he knew it was time to bring it all to a resolution, to an end. The movements suddenly changed, became delayed hard thrusts; there was a scarcely recognisable cry and Mark rubbed harder and harder, afraid to be left behind, to have missed the tide, but suddenly the release, the explosion came, his body shuddered and warm liquid spattered across his chest in an unexpected and welcome caress.

The intensity had gone but the pressure within him

was still there, become an urge to cry as if tears had to be expelled with semen to make the act, the little-understood transformation, complete. He was aware of a towel being placed on his chest and he opened his eyes to see Tony's face, almost disembodied, looking down on him with a smile. 'Use this,' he said and Mark, not quite understanding, made a perfunctory movement to wipe himself dry. Meanwhile he was aware both of a weight within him and Tony's gentle movements to pull away. The discomfort made Mark want to dispel him, but he feared that to do so would irrevocably be to lose part of himself. In an action that was swift and for the first time hinted pain, Tony freed himself, lowered Mark's legs and stretched out beside him.

'You O.K.?' he asked in a voice little more than a whisper.

'Yes.'

'You were great,' said Tony, his arm coming over and pulling Mark to him, dispelling a doubt that had been about to surface.

Mark wanted to kiss him but did not know how Tony would react; instead he put his arm round Tony's shoulders and stared into his eyes.

'We'd better clean up,' Tony said, pulling away and taking the towel to wipe himself. Then they were both on their feet and rearranging blankets and sheets whose age and probable lack of cleanliness were hidden in the gloom. They settled down in each other's arms, stretched out, relaxed, the record player at last turned off. Mark was not even conscious of being tired before he fell asleep.

He was lying flat on his stomach, limbs sprawled, when he was woken by a pleasant but insistent sensation at the base of his spine. Remembering, without making the effort of searching through his memory which would jolt him awake, where he was, he realised that Tony wanted to repeat what they had done the night before. The thought pleased him, was proof not only of his attractiveness but that he had escaped the sterile values of conformity and routine that he had been surrounded by all his life, was a rejection of everything he knew he

55

was supposed to uphold and believe. To be lying here, trusting, defenceless, allowing a stranger to spread his legs, his buttocks, to open him up, to enter him, to move him, to fill him, to transform him, to give him the deepest, strongest and most human sensations possible, was everything, more than everything he might ever want from life. He wanted to stay in this half-sleeping, dream-like state, to float, to be aware of nothing other than what was happening within him; but it was already too late: he could no more fall asleep than he could push Tony off, get up from the bed, put on his clothes and walk calmly out of the door. So he lay there, not wanting to respond, rejoicing in his passivity, wanting to be no more than the object of Tony's desire, no more than the weight, the fullness, the mass of sensation that was filling and flowing over him as intensely as it had done only a few hours before.

Breakfast was tea, old bread and strong margarine, taken as they squatted on the bed. Tony was friendly but not talkative, and Mark was content to look around him, to see in the daylight the stained ceiling, the frayed carpet, the dirty curtains and to accept and admire them as the bohemianism to which he as yet could only aspire. Far from dismaying him, the room's disorder was as warm, comfortable and welcoming as a nest. He could easily see this as home and would happily spend hours sitting in the old armchair looking out at the passing cars and denuded trees, the terraced block opposite and the occasional pedestrian, which all suggested a somehow more meaningful world than the one in which till now he had spent his days.

'I've got to sign on,' Tony said. Mark was not sure what this meant but understood from his tone that Tony wanted to do it alone. 'Where've you got to get back to?'

They talked about the underground and which line Mark would take, stood up to put on jackets and make for the door.

'Haven't left anything, have you?'

'I don't think so. I can always come back for it.' It was the closest Mark could get to talking about meeting again,

56

for he was afraid that if he brought the subject up Tony's only response would be no.

But Tony did invite him back, suggested they meet for a drink at the weekend. Mark went, stood in the pub with him and laughed at the gross jokes from the fat man in drag who was that night's entertainment, but did so with the impatience that came from wanting to be alone with Tony, to make love as they had done before. The room was as he remembered it, the smell and the gloom unchanged; even the love-making was the same, with Mark not dissatisfied but wanting to give more and not knowing what that more might be.

He saw Tony four or five times – meeting at the same bar, drinking for an hour and going back to his room – before the enchantment soured. It was the lack of drive, of energy, of ambition, that Mark felt the keenest, as he came to understand that Tony's days were no more than hours spent watching the small black-and-white television perched on one of the shelves before going out each night to the pub, where he would spend the evening on carefully rationed drinks. In Mark's eyes this inertia harmed him more than Tony, as if Tony's not pulling himself up, not making something of himself (although whatever that something might be, Mark had no idea) reflected more seriously on Mark than on Tony, showing up deficiencies both in his character and his abilities as a lover. Even the dirt and squalor lost its appeal and Mark found himself wanting to clean up, to take the sheets and piles of clothes to the launderette, to paint and put up posters. Finally, Mark felt that Tony's insistence on the same sexual act time after time, no matter how well or lovingly performed, was restrictive and ultimately demeaning in that it did not allow him to explore other, hardly identified aspects of himself. So he had said goodbye to Tony, muttered something about not seeing him for a time and understood that his decision was right when Tony seemed not to understand or not to regret what Mark was telling him.

Now Tony stood a few yards away, drinking, as he

had always drunk, a pint glass from which he would sip at regular, almost timed, intervals. He was alone, and Mark guessed he was looking round him, watching for the next young man like an ageing lion who waits for rather than pursues his prey. It was partly curiosity, partly the satisfaction of knowing he was right, that made Mark want to go up to him, to say hello, to talk and learn that he still lived in the same room, that he still did not work, that the television was perhaps now colour, but that nothing else had changed. He could not, however, for fear that Tony might not recognise him, for fear of the awkwardness of a conversation where they had nothing in common and no reason to be together and for the deeper fear that to go over to Tony would be to go back in time, to become once again the uncertain lonely student he had once been.

Mark turned away, hit by a sudden depression. Time might not wind back but he might become another Tony, perhaps employed, perhaps not short of money, yet coming to this and other bars for the rest of his life, growing older and more lined, more cynical and more morose, longing for a lover and unable to hold one for more than a night. Bars like this, with their apparent camaraderie and sense of security, sucked you in, held you as firmly as a fly in some carnivorous plant, slowly, imperceptibly draining life away. He had to get out before his personality, his individuality, was sucked from him and he became no more than another lonely, ageing man, no longer possessing the unique quality which had attracted Gene and Carl and which was now – God, he hoped still now – holding and fascinating Robert. Indeed Robert was his life-line, his third, last and only chance of escaping and he, Mark, was in danger of throwing it away.

Gulping back the rest of his drink, he made his way as quickly as was compatible with politeness through the crowd towards the door. Outside, his reaction seemed exaggerated, almost laughable, but he had no desire to go back in. Gay bars were a part of his youth, his insecurity; if he wanted Robert he had to turn his back on them, to exchange their false sense of identity for something apparently more fragile but in the end much more dependable – his own strength of character out of which his feelings for Robert, and Robert's respect for him, would surely grow.

Mark walked towards the nearby underground station with no certain idea of where it might take him. It was too early to go home and he did not want to find himself in the middle of crowds in shopping streets looking for clothes or other items he did not really want. He might visit friends, but he could not be sure that his arrival would not be an interruption to a carefully planned day. Besides, he would only want to talk about Robert, as if words, exposing his hurt and confusion, would in themselves heal the wound and have Robert rush back to London and into his arms. His friends, meanwhile, would either listen with genuine sympathy but reveal from their questions and responses that they did not quite understand, that they could say nothing which would ensure Robert's undiminished love, or would pay little attention, change the subject, talk about their own concerns, hardly masking their opinion that Mark's worries were a storm in a tea-cup, that he was only someone else they knew who had lost his head over a pretty but otherwise undistinguished boy.

Yet Robert was anything but undistinguished. It was true that his youth and good looks could easily be a drawback rather than an advantage, leading others older and more cynical to assume that these were his only qualities, but his intelligence, his determination, his belief in himself were rare and much more valuable. He shared not only Gene's dedication to his art but Carl's need to give and take affection and these traits combined gave Mark no choice but to want him, to need him, to love him. From their first meeting Robert had proved himself as Mark's equal, sometimes his superior, his calm seldom ruffled, even the time when they first went to bed.

He had met Robert as promised, at Leicester Square at eight o'clock, nervous, trying not to think of Carl, who was again at work. He suggested the cinema but was happy to agree to a drink, to let Robert lead him to an empty pub in Soho, where they faced each other over a table in the corner furthest from the half-dozen or so other customers. Robert sat over a pint of lager, his black eyes darting out from under the thick black hair that hung like a frozen storm-wave across his forehead, his red shirt curving round his neck and down to his waist, framing a sliver of lightly tanned skin that Mark could not avoid watching. Mark, looking back on this meeting and on every other meeting, could not remember how they began, whether their first words were the mundanities of where each had been and what each had done, or whether they dived at once into the discussions of art and life, of criticism and motivation that swept them along like a raft on a river tumbling over rocks and through canyons on its way to the sea.

It was, Mark calculated, seventy-eight hours since they had first met and fifty-four since they last separated. Although the days were lengthening the time had passed like one long night, darkness in which Robert was no more than a distant memory and Carl a misunderstood and upsetting presence. Nevertheless he had almost hoped that Robert would not appear that evening, would have noticed and been dissuaded by some gaping hole in Mark's personality or his efforts to gloss it over. He would then have waited twenty minutes or half an hour and returned to Carl with a clear conscience and the slight breathlessness of someone who has had a narrow and frightening escape. But Robert had arrived before him, had brought him to this bar, and they were now talking with the ease and intensity of a tennis tournament in which the aim was not to win but to keep the ball in motion, to send it leisurely up into the air or slam it, good-humouredly or mischievously, over the net. No one since Gene had so excited Mark, exhilarated him, made him feel so alive, so full of energy. Then his insecurities had destroyed what he had most wanted to build; now he had the experience and confidence to keep any doubts so deeply buried that they could not be heard. Yet he still did not know whether Robert was gay, nor whether, if he were, he, Mark, would allow himself to seduce or be seduced. He could do nothing, therefore, but talk, could make no movement, no decision that might dissolve the uncertainty into a reality he did not want.

'I've always wanted to dance,' Robert was saying. 'I want to move people, to say for them what they can't say for themselves.'

'So it's not just the glory, the idea of being watched by hundreds of people, a big ego-trip?'

Robert shook his head. 'No. If there are dancers like that I don't know them. You know something? Most dancers are really only dancing for themselves. They only feel alive on stage. They pretend the audience is important; they want to give them a good performance, but when it comes down to it it's only themselves and the others they pay attention to. Technique and style are everything. It's all they can talk about. They're a very inward-looking lot.'

'But you're different,' Mark said, half-teasing.

'Yes, I am. To tell the truth, I don't like dancers much. Just the three or four I know who are good and who want to do the things I want to do.'

'I'd like to see you perform sometime.'

'I'd like you to.' Robert smiled almost tentatively. 'But you can't for a couple of months. We're not doing anything at the academy and the group I'm in has only just started rehearsing.'

'Rehearsing what?'

'A modern piece based on, of all things, Chekhov.'

'What's your. . .' What was the word? 'Role?'

'The soloist.'

Robert's self-mocking smile did not lessen the admiration shading into envy that Mark felt. Nineteen and almost a star; twenty-eight and still struggling to find his own voice.

'Another drink?' Mark offered.

'No thanks. I have a better idea.'

'What?'

'Just round the corner from here is a flat that's empty, that has a double bed and that I just happen to have the keys for.'

'You're tired?' Mark said to mask the sudden exuberance that threatened to explode out of him.

'No,' Robert grinned. 'Not yet. Do you want to go round there?' He looked serious, almost pleading, as if afraid that Mark would refuse. Later Mark realised that in the moment it took him to respond to Robert's suggestion Carl had been no more to him than a shadow of trouble and pain. He had known he should say no to Robert, should leave at once and go home, forget Robert and never see him again, but had also known that he could not, that to do so would be cowardice, would be to close a beckoning door, take the too easy and unthreatening path. Afterwards he was to wonder which of the choices was in fact easier.

'Yes,' he said, 'I do.' The future opened up before him again, dark, unknown, waiting.

They stood up, Robert heaving onto his shoulder the large bag that never seemed to leave him. Outside Mark asked who the flat belonged to, why Robert had the key.

'A friend at college. He's gone away for a couple of days. It's nothing special – just a couple of rooms and a bath – but I thought we could use it.'

The evening was dark, cool rather than cold. People walked past or stood conferring outside restaurants. Traffic was held up as a red Volvo tried to park. The light from an amusement arcade poured out onto the pavement. It all seemed more like a film set than reality. Mark and Robert walked side by side in silence, as if awed by what they were about to do. Mark's mind was blank, a dam shoring up excitement and expectation, fear and recrimination. His footsteps mirrored Robert's slow and measured pace; Mark could not imagine him rushed or hurrying.

The grey door was at the top of a flight of narrow crooked stairs. The room behind it was bare except for cushions scattered on the floor and an enormous, angry abstract painting hanging on one of the walls. Robert dropped his bag, pointed to the bathroom and bedroom, then turned and, unbidden, reached over and let his lips touch Mark's. For a moment they were still, then, more from habit than desire, because it was expected of him rather than what he wanted to do, Mark responded, pressed his mouth against Robert's, dabbed delicately from one corner to the other, felt it give, open to the hardness of his teeth and the softness of his tongue, let his own tongue begin to probe, to stroke, to dance with its partner until, with the rest of their bodies as motionless as if paralysed, they were kissing intently and Mark was fully aware of the strength of desire muffled by Robert's slow movements and deep steady breathing.

'Shall we go into the bedroom?' Robert whispered. Mark nodded, and followed him into a small, equally grey and equally bare room, where the light from a neon sign opposite reflected dully on the upper walls and across the ceiling. He was aware of the brick and darkened windows of the building opposite but had no time to look at them or, as he would otherwise have done, peer down at the pedestrians and passing cars. Robert had his arms round him, had closed his eyes and was kissing him again, so hard that Mark had to respond, to try to enter Robert as he himself was being entered, to push him back gently or allow himself to be pushed over onto the floor.

But why, why, did he feel no desire? Why were his responses no more than reactions, as if there were some failure, a lack of communication so that the part of his body, his brain, his mind, which transformed mere touch and pressure into sexual need, had closed down? And why, when the hardness of Robert's erection pressed against his stomach, did he feel nothing but softness and limpness in his own groin? Why was it that after three days of obsession with Robert, after hours of being fascinated by him, after staring at his eyes, his cheeks, the gentle curve of his neck disappearing under his shirt, after wondering, as urgently as a mystic seeking God, if he would ever kiss, touch, hold, make love with him, did he now feel nothing, like a guest who has eaten is offered an attractive and appetising but quite unwanted meal? He wanted to say stop, no, not today, another time; I'm tired, I'm not in the mood, I want you but . . . but he could not, fearing that Robert would take a rejection today as a rejection for all time, that opportunity's knock did not come twice, that he had no right to withhold from Robert what Robert was so obviously keen to have. All he could do was stay, relax, hope that as they went on the malfunction would repair itself, other circuits would take on the task, and his body would be able to make love with Robert as his mind so desperately wanted to.

They had fallen onto the bed and Robert's hand was pulling Mark's shirt out from under his belt, finding his stomach, pushing slowly up to hold, to grasp his pectorals, while his mouth drifted down his neck. Mark reached down, pulled Robert's tee-shirt up and, Robert lying back for a moment, pulled over his head and off his arms. Then, hoping that action would substitute for the indifference that Robert appeared not yet to have noticed, he gently pushed him back on the bed. In the moment before he leaned over he was aware that Robert's body was as beautifully formed as he had expected, that the muscles of arm and chest, the slenderness of the waist and the light hollow of his stomach were clearly defined but still overlain by the softness of youth. The skin was lightly tanned, hairless except for a few strands at the navel spreading and thickening down towards his belt. He wanted to sit over Robert for hours, watching the faint rise and fall of his breathing, searching for the muffled throb that would reveal his beating heart, committing every detail, every shadow and line to memory so that every aspect of his body would be beside him for the rest of his life, but he knew that Robert expected not the subtle caress of admiration and sight but the grossness of touch, the feel of his hands and mouth. So Mark leaned over, placed his mouth over one nipple as his hand felt for the other, licked it, teased it with his teeth, biting gently until the chest rose and he heard the sudden breath that indicated he had found the right pressure, sucked not only the nipple but the muscle beneath deep into his mouth and felt Robert's whole body move beneath him like a gentle earthquake, his erection pressing into Mark's chest like the insistent begging of a starving child.

But he could not postpone the ensuing stages for ever. Unwillingly he undid Robert's belt, pulled down the zip and eased the trousers out from under his hips as he felt Robert, impatiently, yank his own jeans and underwear down. 'I'm sorry,' he muttered, almost inaudibly, as Robert's head nuzzled into his groin and tried to suck his unresponsive penis into life. There was no response from Robert other than an even fiercer determination to draw Mark into him, to unite them completely.

It had never occurred to Mark that a man's sexual organ could aesthetically appeal to him: when limp it appeared as merely an untidy jumble of skin and hair that interrupted the longer curves of the body; when erect it seemed exaggerated, strained, a caricature of itself like the overdeveloped muscles of body-builders, its attraction much more what it represented, what it offered, than what it was. This penis, however, this apparently sculpted column of flesh, blemish-free, of perfect proportion, smoothness and colour, with its smooth crown and globes sheltering in its foundations, was, in ways he could not understand and did not want to try to understand, indeed beautiful, so much so that he hesitated to touch it, feared that to stroke it with hand or mouth would somehow destroy it, reduce it to the mundane, to no more than the impatient organ of any rutting animal. Yet, he realised, to do nothing would be more wrong, more harmful than to grasp it, for its perfection came from the fact that it was waiting, that it had a purpose to be fulfilled, and slowly, carefully, he kissed and drew it into his mouth.

He was not aware of time passing as they changed position, as his attention shifted here and there on Robert's body. He was aware that there were no curtains, that in the darkness opposite someone might be watching, but the thought did not disturb him; indeed if the unknown figure were somehow benefiting, were made happier or calmer by this display of love, then Mark would welcome him, would want in some way to acknowledge his presence, to draw him in as an unseen partner. That thought, that benevolence, however, was gradually overlain by the deeper worry that his mind, his body, and most importantly his groin were still not responding to Robert's manipulations. He knew – or thought he knew – why, but while he could push the insistent realisation to the back of his mind he could not disguise from Robert what was, or rather was not, happening. 'I'm sorry,' he repeated.

This time Robert heard, drew himself up so they were lying side by side. 'It doesn't matter,' he said.

'It's disappointing for you.'

'Sh.' Robert placed a finger across Mark's lips and eased an arm under his shoulders, bringing them both together. 'If you're cold we can pull up a blanket.'

Mark wasn't cold, but appreciated the pause and that Robert seemed happy for them to be only lying together. He put one arm round Robert, let his other hand rest in Robert's groin and looked down at the body beside him, its graceful tapering to the waist and the strength of its thighs and calves. That action should complement presence he knew and tried to ignore; closing his eyes he tried to drift into a state where he was conscious of no more than himself and the youth beside him, as if in the darkness he found there their two minds might meet and merge, somehow consummate what his body could not.

But the shadow that he had tried to ignore all evening now hung over him more heavily than before. He should turn and face it but he could not – could not, he later realised, reduce it to its components of jealousy and betrayal, love and trust, to awareness of Carl as an entity or even a name. He knew, nevertheless, that the longer he stayed in this room – where, despite everything, he still desperately wanted to be – the ill-feeling would grow stronger, become pain, would force him to get up and dress, would push him out of the flat, down the stairs and into the street, would drive him away from Robert as firmly and remorselessly as the angel expelling Adam and Eve. Before it overcame him he had to give as much as he could, give Robert the pleasure he sought, the pleasure that Mark, in accepting to come here, had promised. Gently disentangling himself, he sat up and leaned over to take Robert's penis in his mouth. Urgently, allowing no distraction, he sucked it back into full erection, found its most sensitive part, its most sensitive rhythm, while Robert lay, almost motionless, either needing this love-making or appreciating Mark's need to give it, allowing the orgasm to build up in him until his body trembled like an awakening volcano and erupted its warm and not entirely welcome liquid into Mark's mouth.

When he had ceased to shudder, Mark drew himself up to lie with Robert's arms round him and his face nuzzled into his chest, his eyes closed as if he were already asleep. Mark stared at the greyness of the ceiling, until Carl, held at bay all evening, finally and without warning broke into his consciousness like a bulldozer demolishing a wall. It was a silent, static image, not even a memory, which in itself implied nothing but which engendered in Mark a deep emotion that hovered between sorrow and guilt.

'I have to go,' he said, gently taking hold of Robert's arm and laying it to the side.

'Why? We can stay the night.'

'You know why. I have a lover who will be waiting for me. I. . .' I shouldn't be here. I shouldn't have done this. It was wrong. But he could not go so far, could not destroy in retrospect Robert's pleasure. 'I have to get back.'

Robert pulled him more tightly, kissed him on the ear, the cheek, the mouth. 'Stay,' he whispered.

'I can't. I want to,' he heard himself say, 'but I can't.' Again he laid aside Robert's arm, stood up and searched on the floor for his clothes. What the fuck have I done, he asked himself, his leg kicking its way into his jeans as he stared at Robert lying across the bed, the hair in his armpits just visible, and the roundness of his buttocks with their paler patch of skin inviting him to caress, to kiss them. I'm with someone I don't want to leave and I have to go home to someone else who loves me and whom I love and owe all my affection and loyalty. I want Robert, I need him; Carl needs me and I want him. I want both. I shouldn't be here; I should have told Robert no, should have left him in the pub and gone home, walked, if necessary, walked off the energy, let the night air blow away the desire. But I couldn't. Because there was, there is, something about Robert so wonderful, so compelling, I could not, I could never refuse.

'Hey,' he said when he was dressed. 'I'm going.'

Robert pushed himself onto his side, as bleary-eyed as

if he had been asleep. His penis, still semi-erect, flopped over his thigh; Mark wanted to hold it, to touch it again. If he begged me to stay, pleaded and abased himself, it would make it much easier to reject him, to see him as no more than a pouting teenager, a child wanting his toy. His calmly accepting the situation, without complaint, makes me want him even more.

'Call me tomorrow. In the afternoon,' Robert said. 'I've got some time off; I'll be home then.'

It was too late to pretend that the evening had not happened or that Mark was able to put it behind him, to return to Carl, to forget that he had ever met this naked figure who lay watching him, whom he wanted more and more. 'O.K.,' he said, leaning over to kiss Robert, wanting and not allowing himself to run a hand through his hair.

The stairs were dark. He walked down them slowly as if they were leading him somewhere new, into a different world from the one he had left not long before. The street was bright and busy; his watch told him it was still early, that he would be home long before Carl. He walked to the underground station as acutely conscious of Robert as if he were still with him, as if he were once again apologising for his lack of response, or lying beside him, slowly falling asleep. On the train, however, Robert faded from his mind, was replaced by Carl, now a stranger, scarcely recognisable as the lover he lived with. The train rattled on and the future gaped before him, drew him on, dark and vast as a black hole.

TWO

I

'To us,' Mark raised his glass once the waiter had poured the wine and walked away. 'Two months down. Who knows how long to go?'

'To us. And a merry Christmas.' Carl drank, his eyes fixed on Mark. 'I love you, you know.'

'I know,' Mark smiled. 'I love you too.'

'Thank you, *Capital Gay*.'

'Don't thank them. I didn't want them to send anyone attractive.'

'You didn't?'

'No. Everyone warned me against sleeping with the lodger. David said I'd start doing little favours and end up not charging any rent. You – or whoever he was – would just take advantage, use my tea-bags and everything.'

'Oh, no! That would be terrible.'

'Have you?' Mark asked.

'Have I what?'

'Used my tea-bags?'

'I'm afraid so. Will you kick me out?'

'No,' said Mark, suddenly serious. 'Never.'

'Don't say that. Not unless you mean it.'

'I like this place,' Carl went on, looking round at the other tables set at discreet distances. The lighting was dim and the waiters quietly polite. 'We ought to come again.'

'After another couple of months. And you haven't tried the food yet.'

'Next week if it's good.'

'Next week? I can't afford that.'

'You're always worrying about money,' Carl complained. 'Don't. There's always more.'

'Not in my line of work. And I have a mortgage to feed.'

'With me helping you feed it. Does the bank know?'

'I'm not prepared to answer on the grounds that it would certainly incriminate me.'

'I wanted you to be good-looking,' Carl said suddenly.

'Bad luck. Why?'

'Because of the sound of your voice over the telephone.'

'What about it?'

'I thought it was wonderful. Deep and strong. Confident.'

'Really? What did I say?'

'Not much. You just gave me the address and told me how to get there and said that a couple of others were already on their way.'

'One didn't turn up.'

'And the other?'

'Had less personality than the neighbour's cat. So, tell me more. What did you think when I opened the door?'

'There was this weird guy who talked a bit too much. I think you were nervous. You sat me down in the kitchen and asked me all these questions about what I did and where I came from and how long I'd been in London. If it'd been anyone else I would have said it was none of their business.'

'Why not me?'

'I liked you.'

Mark stored that remark in his memory with the greed of a tramp pocketing a coin. 'When you came in I thought, Wow! I want him! But there was a little voice at the back of my mind saying, don't let him move in; it'll only cause problems, and a loud voice at the front of my mind – and further down my body – saying yeah, yeah, give him the room, give him the room.'

'It's a good thing you listened to the right voice.'

'There really wasn't any choice. I certainly wasn't going to let the other guy have it and I needed someone to move in as soon as possible.'

'Thanks.'

'Not at all,' Mark said. 'Tell me when you first wanted to go to bed with me.'

'The moment I saw you.'

'Three days it took you. Why so long?'

'Close your eyes!'

'They're closed,' Mark insisted. 'But if you don't finish what you're doing in thirty seconds. . .'

'All right, you can open them. Merry Christmas!'

'What?' Set out before him on the table were a bottle of champagne, two glasses, toast on a plate, a small opened tin that he suspected contained caviar, a dish of apparently home-made chocolates, various packets wrapped in coloured paper and, standing to the side, watching in apprehension and eagerness, Carl.

'This . . . it's wonderful.' Indeed it was. No one had ever done this much for him, whether at Christmas or at any other time. 'Thank you. Thank you, lover. A lot.'

'Don't I get a kiss?' Carl pretended to pout.

'Of course you do. Come over here.' Mark reached over, put an arm round his neck and brought him to sit on his lap. 'You know something? You're incredible. And I love you.'

'Happy New Year!' The words bounced around the room like the lights reflected in the mirrors, to be swiftly drowned out by the overloud strains of a record of Auld Lang Syne. Mark found himself trying, like all those around him, to remember the words, as one of his hands was grasped by a girl of about eighteen tottering on tall narrow heels and wearing a low-cut dress that revealed anaemic breasts, and the other was gripped by a man younger than himself sporting a loud tie over a belly that threatened to burst through his shirt. Gazing across the dance-floor, where the brightness was as thick as fog, he caught sight of Carl, incongruously but attractively elegant in his white shirt and blue bow-tie, standing between Arthur – the manager – and Ellen, whose job it apparently was to stand at the door, look beautiful and take care of the more freely spending guests. Carl winked at him and extended an already broad smile, then turned his attention back to those he was with and said something which made Ellen almost collapse in laughter. Because Carl was

71

enjoying himself, was so obviously at ease and happy, Mark was content to be here, to be polite, to try to be friendly to people he neither knew nor wanted to know. It was an effort and he wondered whether Arthur and Ellen and the rest of the staff knew who he was, knew that Carl was gay and if not, if intuition suddenly told them, would the atmosphere change, would they become distant, even hostile and ask them to leave? He was being paranoid, he knew; the risk was minimal and worth the opportunity to see where Carl worked, to see that he had a life and identity which was separate and in no way dependent on Mark. For Mark had begun to suspect that he meant everything to Carl, that Carl had forgotten the few friends he had in London and would be happy doing no more than spending all of every day with him, which made him afraid that he was not strong enough, that there was not enough of him to maintain his own sense of identity and satisfy Carl. It had not been a problem until the school holidays began, but for the last ten days they had not been out of each other's presence for more than an hour and that had created a newer, deeper intimacy which Mark enjoyed but was nevertheless wary of.

The music had stopped and the disc-jockey was saying something unintelligible. Mark was aware that the girl beside him was waiting to be kissed, the next and, he hoped, final part of the New Year ritual. He put on a smile and with a touch of roughness that he hoped disguised his natural reluctance bent over to graze her lips.

'Who's it from?' he asked, seeing Carl's concentration as he read.

'Edwin.'

Mark was surprised, had taken the name and the person to be forgotten. 'What's he saying?'

'He misses me.'

'Oh.' Mark wanted to lean over, skim the lines, sift the words for any. . . any what? Danger? 'Do you miss him?'

'Sometimes.'

'And I don't make up for it?'

'Of course you do.' Carl looked up, almost petulant. 'But. . . let me finish this, please.'

Mark said nothing. He stared at the paper in Carl's hand.

The flat was empty when he arrived home from school. He was surprised, not sure whether to be worried or put out, for he had grown accustomed to Carl greeting him, his smile sometimes masking ill-temper if the evening meal was not progressing. No longer feeling guilty that Carl was happy to cook for him, recognising that it was not a service which had to be paid for in some other way, this absence, this break with tradition disturbed him and he did not know what to think or what to do.

To occupy himself he made tea and took it through to the living-room, where he anaesthetised his thoughts watching television. An hour passed before the telephone rang.

'Mark?'

'Where are you?'

'The Royal Oak.' Carl's voice wavered between aggression and apology.

'What are you doing there?'

'Oh, I've been having a good time.'

'You should've left a note. I was worried.'

'You don't sound it.'

'I was.'

'O.K., O.K., you were worried.'

He's drunk, Mark realised. What time is it? Half past six? Seven?

'Can you come over here?' Carl went on.

'Why?'

'Because I've no money. I can't get home. I thought you'd like to come and have a drink and then we could go out somewhere for a meal.'

'Aren't you working tonight?'

'No, it's my day off.'

'Carl, it's been a long day. I'm not in the mood. I can't afford it.'

'Come on, you old meanie, of course you can afford it.

Or lend me the money and I'll take you out and pay you back on Friday.'

For a moment he was attracted, but they had gone out too often, sat in too many quiet and ultimately character-less restaurants for him to want to put on his shoes and jacket and leave the flat again. 'No, Carl, not tonight. Come on home.'

'I don't want to come home. I want to enjoy myself.'

'Well. . .'

'Oh, fuck off. I'll see you later.'

The front door was closed more loudly than usual, waking Mark up rather than momentarily disturbing his sleep. The sound of running water in the bathroom was followed by a long silence. At last the bedroom door opened and he heard Carl come in, knock against the desk and whisper 'Fuck!' The clothes were dropped on the floor rather than quietly folded and put on the chair and, instead of his usual tiptoe, Carl stumbled over to the bed, lifted up the covers and flopped in, his arm roughly falling over Mark's shoulders.

'Are you all right?' Mark whispered.

'Yeah, yeah. Great. Everything's fucking great.' His breath was heavy with alcohol.

Mark turned, partly concerned and partly irritated by being awake in the middle of the night before another long teaching day. 'What's wrong?' he asked.

'Nothing's wrong. I've just lost my job, that's all. It happens all the time in this business.'

'Lost your job?'

'Yeah. Remember I told you Arthur was leaving? He left. We have a new manager and the new manager doesn't like me. Or maybe he doesn't like poufs. He's going to change the image, he says. Brighten the place up a bit, have a few more girls in mini-dresses and a few less men like me. I don't fit the new image. I can go at the end of the week. Fine, I said, I'll go, but you're making a mistake – I'm the best bloody barman you've got.'

'You'll find another job, won't you?'

'That's not the fucking point. I want *that* job. I made that place and that bastard's got no right to fire me.'

Mark felt helpless, did not know what to say. 'Maybe he'll change his mind.'

'He won't change his mind. Oh, for fuck's sake, you don't know anything about the business. He's a new manager and every new manager always gets rid of the old staff and brings in his friends. I'll go back there in a month and nothing'll have changed except there'll be someone who doesn't know a Spritzer from a Campari wearing my bow tie and standing at my place in the bar and John'll say he hopes I've found somewhere else and if I haven't he can offer me a job washing dishes in the kitchen.'

'Maybe he is going to change the image.'

'Christ, you don't understand!' Carl sat up, switched on the light, dazzling Mark. 'I've worked bloody hard for that place. The customers like me; I do my job well and at the end of it I just get kicked out. If anyone should be manager it should be me. I could run that place better and cheaper than anyone. But don't you worry. You've got your nice little teaching job and you're there for the rest of your life as long as you don't go ga-ga or grope the pretty boys. What the fuck do you know about it? What the fuck do you care?'

The words hurt, were almost incomprehensible, but they hurt. 'I care because I love you.'

Carl snorted. 'Forget it. Let's get to sleep.'

Mark put out his arm, but Carl wordlessly pushed it away.

'Carl, we can't afford it.'

'Not again! I'm tired of you telling me what we can and can't afford. It's one bottle of whisky, that's all. If I go into a pub and drink a bottle's worth it's going to cost four, five times this. So this is cheap, right? And I'll pay for it. It's my money.'

'Then who's going to pay for the food?' Mark was conscious of the other customers passing, stopping to choose from the shelves he and Carl were standing near.

He wondered if they were listening to what was being said.

'Oh, fuck!' Carl slammed the bottle so hard into the trolley Mark feared it would break. 'I can't stand this. I can't stand being told what I can and can't have. You're just like my father going on at me. "You can't do this and you can't do that." I came away to London to get away from all that and now you're going on at me just like him. I'm going home. Do what the fuck you want, buy what the fuck you want, but I'm going home.'

Mark watched Carl walk away, push roughly past a queue at one of the tills and thrust open the door into the street. He did not know whether to run after him, nor what he might say, what he should have said or what he could do. With a weight inside him as dull as a pain he pushed the half-filled trolley onwards, wondering, now that Carl had left with the shopping list, what he should buy.

'So you love me. How does that get me a job in the middle of March anywhere except a crummy pub where they pay starvation wages? Leave me alone. You can't help. I'm going to bed.'

'I'm going home. I'm going back up North. As soon as I've saved enough.'

'There's no food. I wasn't in the mood. Anyway, it's your turn to cook.'

'I'll get drunk if I want to get drunk. Can't you stop telling me what to do?'

Some days Mark considered asking Carl to leave. His love had shrunk, confronted too often by a hostility which seemed less a rejection than an indifference. He felt powerless, unable to help Carl, unable to relieve his anger, unable even to sympathise, for he could not understand why Carl would not at least take part-time or temporary work until he found another club where the hours and tips were what he wanted. There were times when it seemed that there was a gulf between them so great that it could not be measured or bridged, that whatever had brought and held them together in the first few months had, unseen and without warning, come apart, dissolved, left them standing alone on their islands of solitude. Yet even at his lowest Mark could not bring himself to say all right, go back to Oldham or Bolton or wherever you came from, stop insulting me and shouting at me, get out if you're so unhappy here, for there were still some good moments together: evenings when Carl took pride in producing a meal and they sat in the kitchen or the living-room, or when Carl asked him to play some of his music and sang the words dreadfully out of key, weekend afternoons when they would take a long walk over Primrose Hill or Hampstead Heath and Carl would talk about his childhood and his family, and try to explain the complex emotions he felt. These remnants of warmth and togetherness, unwillingness to send away the only lover that had lived with him and fear that no one might take his place persuaded Mark that if their relationship was to end there would come a point when it became so unbearable that Carl would make his own decision to go.

Meanwhile, as if all his energy, all his love, were channelled into accepting and keeping Carl beside him, Mark found that he wanted no sex with Carl, no physical contact other than the occasional kiss. Each night when they went to bed, the hour a compromise between Mark's need to get up early and Carl's habit of staying up late, he wanted only to fall asleep. If Carl's hand should rest, not on his shoulder but on his thigh, slowly feeling its way higher and deeper until it grasped his shrinking penis or tried to probe gently between his buttocks, he could not prevent himself from tensing or his breath from halting and he would have to resist the urge to fling Carl's hand away, as outraged as if he was being touched by an unwelcome stranger. He did not understand why he reacted in this way: he knew that Carl's reaching out was both his need and apology, his seeking reassurance that Mark still loved him; but he could not force himself to want Carl, to be aroused by the slightly chubby body with the coarse skin that only weeks ago he had been making love to every day. He could only whisper ungraciously 'I don't want to', push Carl's hand to the side if he insisted and drift warily off into sleep, knowing that the next day, the next night would be the same.

II

'Write.'

'I will.'

They were silent for a moment. Gene sat at an angle on his stool, his left arm resting on the counter beside the coffee he had ordered and not drunk. Mark glanced at the clock; it had advanced another minute. When the hand moved again it would be time for him to pick up his bags and walk out and onto the platform.

'I really don't want to go.' He tried to laugh.

Gene said nothing. His expression was stiff and his eyes were cold; he was attempting, Mark realised, not to cry.

'Hey, maybe I'll be back. Give me two or three weeks to sort things out, see how I feel.'

Gene forced a smile, eased off his stool. 'I'm going to go.'

'A man's gotta do what a man's gotta do.' The humour and caricatured American accent drew a weak smile.

They put their arms round each other on the concourse and slid kisses into each other's necks. Mark wanted to prolong the embrace but Gene was already breaking away. 'Have a good trip,' he said, his voice barely audible above the station hubbub. He turned and walked towards the metro, a tall, slim figure in a dark blue jacket whose slow gait and stiffness seemed to express the deep and bright emotion Mark felt. Then he turned the corner by the newsagent's stand and Mark was alone, no more than another tired tourist at the end of his holiday. Coldly, his feelings and thoughts suddenly frozen, he walked towards his train.

'Will you accept the charges for a call from France?'

'From France? Of course.' If he hesitated it was because he had not expected to hear so soon.

'Mark?'

'Gene! How are you?'

'O.K.! How are things with you?'

'The same as ever. There are exams coming up at school.'

'I got your letter,' Gene said, his voice apparently emotionless, making Mark hesitate, wonder what he was going to say.

'And?'

'I've thought about you a lot since you left. About you – and your body.'

Bahdy; the American pronunciation made the word different, as if it were divorced from Mark himself. 'And. . . ?' Mark prompted, knowing but not yet believing what would come next.

'Do you want to come back?'

'Of course I want to come back. Why do you think I wrote to you?'

'I guess I want you to come back too. I've really missed you. It's strange; I haven't felt like this about anyone for a long time. I thought I was quite happy being alone.'

'But you're not. And I'm not. When do you want me to come?' It surprised him, yet he found it natural that everything could be so simple.

'Whenever you can.'

'This Friday?'

'So soon?'

'Well, if you want me to put it off. . .'

'No,' said Gene, for the first time a note of warmth, of urgency in his voice.

'I can get the last flight.'

'You're coming by plane?'

It was expensive but well worth the extra hours spent

79

with Gene rather than alone on the boat and the train. As the plane rose into the air it seemed to take with it only the better parts of Mark, the confident song-writer, the generous lover, leaving behind the schoolteacher, his petty routine and doubts. With the gin and tonic that gave him a swift sensation of lightness, of competence and power, he toasted his new self, the one who lived in London but commuted to his lover in Paris, who was an intelligent and successful performer, who found nothing too difficult, who could approach every situation with thought and care. He briefly inspected the man who was sitting beside him reading a magazine, a plain gold ring on his wedding finger, and glanced over to the French couple talking across the aisle. He was now one of them, an international traveller in their league, but luckier; he had Gene.

'Let's see what you've been working on.'
'No,' said Gene.
'Come on.'
'No.'
'Why not?'
'Because the work has to be all mine. I don't want any comments from anyone else until it's done.'
'At least tell me what it is.'
'It's a portrait. Of Leila.'
'She asked for it?'
'No. I asked to paint her. She has a wonderfully dark and angular face.'
'What do you hope to do with it?'
'I don't want to talk about it,' Gene insisted.
'I'm sorry.'
'Don't you feel the same about your songs?' Gene asked. 'You don't want anyone to influence them? You want them to be all yours?'
'Yes,' Mark admitted, aware that he let himself be influenced, let his music follow familiar patterns, let even his lyrics be triggered by others' ideas. 'But I haven't yet found my own voice; I still need to learn from others.'
'Learn the techniques, yes, but not the style, what you

want to say. But. . .' Gene stopped, laughed. 'I'm falling into my own trap. And I haven't even heard what you sing. Why didn't you bring a tape?'

'I haven't got one. And I wasn't sure you'd be interested.'

'I am. Make one. I don't mean in a studio. Just at home. Stick a microphone in front of you.'

'I will. And I'll send it to you, I promise.'

They had started laughing in the first ten minutes when they overheard a woman ('from Kansas' Gene guessed from the accent) pointing out to her husband the Louvre as Noter Dayme and from that moment everything had been funny, from the guide's monotonous commentary to the German with the video camera for whom every shot began with his wife and daughter in close-up and panned at the same speed and angle to whichever sight, famous or not, they were passing. When he stood at the front of the boat pointing his camera towards them like the death-ray of an old science-fiction film, and shouted down the aisle in his own language and heavily-accented English that they should all wave at him and smile, Mark whispered to Gene, 'No, not the home movie! Anything, even the comfy chair, but not the home movie,' and they collapsed against each other giggling like schoolgirls.

Their laughter did not make the trip on the *bateau-mouche* any less romantic and even through the distorted lens of humour Mark could see the grandeur of much that was being pointed out to him. It was all three-dimensional, unlike the streets and museums of other towns that he had wandered through alone or with companions that he had no more in common with than that they had both chosen this holiday at the same time. It was as if Gene, by sitting, talking and laughing here beside him, were infusing everything around him with his personality, was making it all inexplicably alive.

'What do you mean, everything has a purpose? You've said that before.' They were walking through the Jardins du Luxembourg, one couple amongst many, amongst groups of students and families enjoying the spring sunshine.

'I think there's more to us than being born, waking up each morning and eventually dying.'

'A soul? An after-life? Heaven or hell?'

'You could put it like that, but I don't think of it that way.'

'How do you think of it?'

'I don't know. Sometimes I'm aware of something else, a strength, a force; I don't know what you'd call it.'

'God?'

'Maybe.' Gene shrugged. He seemed reluctant to speak but Mark was curious, wanted to see and understand more of this facet of his character. He had never thought about religion, had, when the topic came up, swept aside as impossible any notion that he and those around him were any more than complex collections of molecules that would disintegrate in a predictable time-span. If Gene, however, as intelligent and thoughtful as he was, claimed that life was more, then Mark could only listen and half believe that it was true.

'A force to do what?' he asked.

'To be ourselves, more fully ourselves.'

'How do we become aware of it?'

'Maybe we don't. Maybe only a few are. It's nothing special, nothing important.'

But it was. If Gene had something, a sixth sense, an ability to see or understand what Mark could not, it made Mark inferior, a second-rate citizen, a beta longing to be an alpha. Even worse, when Gene understood that Mark lacked what he took for granted, he would lose interest, see Mark as no more than a pleasant companion and gradually put him aside in favour of another. Mark shuddered, and wondered how he could learn more without revealing his own inadequacy.

'When did you first become aware of it?'

'I don't remember. When I was about fifteen or sixteen. Some nights I used to lie awake and there'd be an incredibly powerful sensation, like . . . like an electric current gripping my body, but not painful, more like pressure.

And when it passed it seemed that I understood things, understood the world much better. I used to get mad at my parents but when it happened I knew that it wasn't their fault; it was just the way things were and I shouldn't let it bother me. It still happens occasionally, but not so much. Maybe I don't need it any more.'

'That's all it is, just pressure?'

'No.' Gene shook his head. 'It's much much more. . . I can't explain it. But it reassures me. It tells me that nothing is really important, that all I have to do is concentrate on my painting.'

'And what about me?'

'What about you?'

Don't you have to concentrate on me? 'Will I never have this . . . this awareness?'

'I don't know. Does it matter? It's only my own peculiarity.'

Gene had not been keen but Mark persuaded him to sketch him. He sat by the window, looking down into the street, occasionally glancing, as far as his motionless face would allow him, at the bed where Gene sat, legs crossed, sketching with slow, broad movements. He wanted to talk but Gene only answered his questions perfunctorily, and he fell into silence, looking out and down at the scene below. People walked past more hurriedly than at night, but the Arabs from the supermarket opposite had brought their conversation out into the street and were talking as animatedly and good-humouredly as ever. One or two restaurants were closed, apparently deserted, while those which were open seemed to do little business. I'd love to live here, Mark told himself. To have a piano against that wall and to spend the morning composing, going out when I had finished a song or found myself getting nowhere, to have a drink in the café around the corner that overlooks the Seine. And Gene would paint, except that I'd probably drive him wild repeating the same phrases again and again. We'd need to get a bigger flat, one that had a sound-proofed piano room or a studio far away down a long corridor; we could have an internal phone system so I could call him up and say hey, lover, do you want a break? Shall we go for a walk? Or just go to the café? And we'd become famous and he'd do the covers for all my albums and when they interviewed me I'd make certain they knew that I lived with, was the lover of Gene Crewe. We'd grow old together and travel the world and eventually move away from Paris and have a house on the Mediterranean and all these famous painters and musicians would come and stay with us. And we'd go to America and I'd meet his parents and they'd really like me and Gene would discover that he loved his Dad after all. It would be wonderful, really wonderful.

He was disappointed by the portrait, saw in it no great depth, no special talent. It could have been drawn by any of the artists who sketched tourists outside the National Portrait Gallery and in Shaftesbury Avenue. But he told Gene he liked it and Gene shrugged as if disclaiming any responsibility for the paper now in Mark's hands.

'Then, although everyone else in the class said he was wrong, he claimed that I'd told them the title was "The Jester *Is* Shakespeare" and he wasn't going to rewrite it. When I read it I had to admit it was really quite good. But I shall be very glad when he leaves. He's way above me and he knows it.'

'I'd like to see you teach,' Gene said.

'I don't teach. I entertain. I keep my classes amused for forty minutes. . . That doesn't mean they learn anything. I've got fourteen-year-olds who can't even spell four-letter words. All I'm doing is keeping them happy so they won't bully each other, threaten me or carve up the school property too much.'

'Don't you enjoy it?'

Mark considered. 'I don't mind it when I'm actually teaching. Most of my classes are taking English as an option and are actually interested in what they're doing; I only have a couple of third forms who are doing it compulsorily. I keep them happy by going for what I think will interest them. What I hate is everything that goes on outside the classroom – the correction, the staff meetings, the lunch supervision, the union. I don't want to know anything about it.'

'I'm not sure I believe you,' Gene said. 'I get the impression you're a pretty good teacher.'

'Don't. Don't say that. I don't want to be. The last thing I want to do is find myself there in ten, twenty years' time. At least the pupils get out after a few years, while we're stuck there. It's like an open prison where everything gets older and greyer and dirtier. There's one old woman who's been there for thirty years and all she can talk about is school and the good old days when smoking in the toilets was the most serious offence imaginable. I've no intention of ending up like that.'

'Then don't. Get out.'

'I will,' Mark said, the promise seeming that much stronger, more certain to be fulfilled, because he was making it to Gene. 'I will.'

Gene did not like to be fucked – Mark hated the word but accepted the inevitability of its use. He had let it happen before to please Mark but this time he quietly and apologetically said no. Nor did he wish to fuck Mark. Sometimes, Gene said, he liked love-making to be rough and aggressive but not violent or painful. Mark was willing, even excited, to kneel over Gene, to trap him between his thighs, hold him down stretched out like a sacrifice, a toy, or to find himself pinned to the floor and looking up at the thin but muscular body which dominated him, which forced its cock into his mouth and nearly choked him; but he found these actions and the motivation behind them more a diversion than an end in themselves, amusement and play which were an inadequate substitute for the affection he wanted to express.

Leaving a second time was not difficult. It was almost jauntily that Mark kissed Gene goodbye before he boarded the train to the airport, knowing that the separation was not permanent, that in four, three, perhaps two weeks he would be back, the routine established of a series of visits which would become closer and longer until he was living permanently with Gene. Indeed, the fact that they could part, that each recognised the other had his own life to lead, was proof of their maturity, of their mutual respect, made their time together much more meaningful and valuable.

'Make that tape and send it to me,' Gene said.

'I will. You'll have it by next Monday at the latest. And I want to see that portrait of Leila.'

'Thanks for coming.'

'Don't thank me. I came because I wanted to. And I'm coming again and again.'

'You'd better get on the train.'

I love you. No, it was too soon; Gene would take neither the words nor him seriously. 'Goodbye.'

The night was black. Mark stared through the narrow window, straining for a view of the lights of Dunkirk. It would be better to doze, to try to sleep, but he suspected that to close his eyes and extend the darkness would somehow be to extend the journey and postpone their docking by many hours. He would have to sleep on the train to Paris if he was not to arrive so exhausted that the day, half his time with Gene, was ruined. Then, he knew, although he tried to ignore it, on Sunday there would be the same long journey back to London and he would arrive at school baggy-eyed and unshaven, depressed from having left Gene and with neither the energy nor the will to teach.

It was something he was going to have to get used to. The air fare was an extravagance he could seldom afford and half-term and the holidays came too infrequently for him to stay longer than a weekend. But as long as Gene would not, could not, come to London, Mark would have to resign himself to weeks made doubly busy by exams and all the telephone calls, letter-writing and appointments that arose from buying his flat and weekends with Gene or packing and catching up with washing and all the other minor but important activities that would otherwise never get done. Meanwhile his back ached and his legs were uncomfortably splayed out – while Gene was almost certainly asleep, stretched out on the mattress, to wake in the morning refreshed and well-rested. Had he spent the last fortnight thinking about Mark as intensely as Mark had thought about Gene? When he was not painting, not concentrating on shape and texture and colour, was it Mark and the wish to have Mark present that he was conscious of? Probably not, and there were implications in that answer that Mark did not want to contemplate.

They had gone back to the restaurant where they had eaten the first night they had met. The waiters were the same but did not recognise them, did not treat them as the anniversary couple Mark considered them to be. The day had been long; he had little more than dozed in the train and only slept for an hour in the afternoon on their return from another of the long walks that Gene liked to take. They had not talked much, Mark being too tired and Gene seemingly not in the mood, but as the meal and the evening progressed and they drank first one bottle of wine then ordered another, their conversation developed, broadened and deepened, with Mark consciously trying to learn more about Gene, his background and his thoughts. Gene's answers, however, were vague; his past, he claimed, irrelevant, his present thoughts seldom put into words. As for his art; 'I try not to analyse,' he said. 'If you take things apart you end up with nothing. What's the point?'

'To understand,' said Mark, 'to be able to paint or write or whatever it is you want, better.'

'Don't you kill it? If you worked out that the chords you write make that sound because they are setting up certain vibrations wouldn't that mean you stopped producing music and just drew up combinations of vibrations? You wouldn't hear what you were doing because you'd be too busy making sure it was mathematically accurate. I don't want to know that I can put laughter in someone's eyes simply by setting them at a particular angle. If you follow that line you end up with a dead art or a prescribed art – and that's even worse.'

'O.K., that may be true. But what I want is to understand *you* better. Doesn't it help to ask about your family and school and the people you've been in love with before?'

Gene shook his head. 'Why? I'm me, here and now. Why don't you just learn how to be with me now rather than ask, ask, ask about the past?'

Mark was certain he had a point to make, if only he could find the right words to express it. 'What about if one of us is unhappy or we argue? Doesn't it help to talk it over, to talk it out?'

'It might. But who's unhappy? Are you? I'm not.'

'No, but. . .' As often with Gene, Mark found himself at the dead end of his own argument. 'So you like my songs,' he said, changing the subject as Gene poured out more wine.

'Yes. You've got talent. I'm surprised you haven't gone into the business full-time.'

The words were good to hear, but were not enough. He needed more, some tangible proof of his ability, of his future success. 'I can't.'

'Why not?'

'I can't afford it. What if I fail?'

'That's the risk you have to take.'

'But these songs are exceptions. I don't know if I can produce more. It's different for you. You know you can take photographs, you can paint, you've got whatever it takes. I don't. I'm always afraid that the last song I've written is the last I'll ever write, that it may please me but no one else'll like it.'

'What do you think?' Gene said, his eyes cold, almost hostile. 'That I never worry? That all I need to do is splatter paint onto the canvas and it'll make a perfect picture? Do you know how many paintings I've sold? Five, and all of them to friends helping me out. I may never sell another painting in my life. I have no guarantees. No one's going to pick me up if I fall. So don't tell me about your doubts and your worries. We all have them; they're nothing special. Just go home and sit down and write. Find yourself an agent or a producer or whatever it is you need. And if the first isn't interested, try another and another and another until you find someone who recognises how good you are. But don't go on about how difficult it all is. We all know that.'

Mark was silent, shocked by the appearance of this new, angry Gene, wondering whether he had gone too far, distanced himself too much.

'Do you want some more wine?' Gene asked, calm again. 'I really want to get drunk.'

III

'He's gone.' Mark looked round the living-room and realised that he was indeed alone, that Carl was not just out of sight, in the bathroom or preparing food in the kitchen, would not suddenly push the door open, say something and fall silent as he saw that Mark was on the telephone. He wondered why he felt nothing, as if when Carl packed he had not only taken clothes from wardrobe and drawers but ripped Mark's emotions from his mind and stuffed them into his cases, as compensation, a trophy, a souvenir to take back north with him.

'Oh.' Robert's voice told him nothing.

'Well, can we meet?'

'Not until late. We're starting rehearsals.'

'That's O.K. What time?'

'Ten? In Duke's Road?' Underlying the wariness in Robert's voice was the enthusiasm Mark had known.

'I'll be there.' Like a trickle along a dried-up stream, sensation gradually returning to a numbed limb, hope, an echo of the excitement of a few days before, seeped into Mark's mind.

'Don't you have to work tomorrow?'

'Does it matter?'

'I've missed you,' Robert said after a pause. 'I wanted to call, but. . .'

With that admission the full force of emotion flooded

through Mark, as welcome as water to a man dying of thirst. 'But you couldn't. I know. It wouldn't have helped.'

Robert was silent, as if he could think of nothing to say. Nor did Mark want to speak, for it would only be to talk about Carl and that was a wound too fresh, too raw to be touched. 'I'd better get back to the correction I'm doing,' he lied. 'I'll see you at ten.'

Mark's chin rested lightly on Robert's shoulder as he watched him brush his teeth and swill water around and out of his mouth. He stared at Robert's eyes in the mirror, saw the sadness that often seemed to linger there. 'Hey,' he said, 'smile.' Robert grinned, spat for the last time and replaced the toothbrush – the one Mark had bought for him – on the shelf. It was when he turned to face Mark, to wait, to give him all his attention, to look at him with patience and a curiosity that verged on wonder that Mark finally accepted that Robert was indeed here, in his home, a few inches away from him, that everything that had prevented them from being together had been swept aside or had never existed; that he, they, were at the start of something which might resemble what had gone before but would be quite different, that for the first time he felt confident to handle whatever difficulties might present themselves, that the days and months spent with Gene and Carl, even the few hours passed with forgotten strangers, had prepared him, qualified him for what was about to begin. He leaned forward, kissed Robert, let his tongue push under Robert's lips, between his teeth, let it explore Robert's mouth and taste the toothpaste that seemed to be as much a part of him and therefore as arousing as the faint smell of sweat that Mark had already begun to recognise. He let his arms come round Robert's back, and pull the two of them gently together, no longer desperate to squeeze him tightly, to try through pressure to meld them into one body, for he recognised that Robert was not part of Mark but another separate, independent individual, which was how it should be, how Mark wanted it to be. Most important of all, as their bodies met, rested against each other as if magnetised, Mark's erection caressing Robert's through the muffling of underwear and trousers was as strong, his desire as deep, as it had ever been and the final doubt, the worry that at this moment something might go wrong, that today would be like the last time and tomorrow would follow, that he would never be able to make love with Robert, melted away.

The room was bright, cold. He squatted in a corner trying to make himself inconspicuous, watching the dancers before him and reflected in the mirror, tubular in their leotards, identifiable as much by the different bright colours as by the shape of their bodies or the way they held themselves. They stood, not quite motionless, sparking into life with the notes from the piano and dying as the music stopped and the middle-aged woman with unkempt hair stepped forward and moved one or other into a slightly different position or said no, it would look better another way, and they all resumed their positions like puppets waiting for the strings to be tugged again.

Robert had smiled at him when he came in, but since then had paid him no more attention, had listened to the woman when she spoke, smiled once or twice at his partners, but seemed to be aware less of his surroundings than of an inner voice or music. Mark watched him, tried to compare him objectively with the others, but the choreographer was more interested in positions than in dancing, in having each remember what the movements were between A and B rather than how well they were performed. Nevertheless it seemed to Mark that Robert moved with more grace than the others, as it also seemed that he was the most attractive of the men; although tights and tee-shirts complimented and drew attention to other slim and muscular bodies, his eyes did not wander: it was only Robert he wanted to see. He wondered if it was here that Robert spent his days, his body one of a graceful line, dipping, bending, his leg outstretched, straight or curved, his arm a semi-circle above his head, not so much a dancer as a platonic ideal of masculinity, of movement.

It was surely a different, higher plane of existence that Robert, all dancers, lived on, touching the ordinary world of nine-to-five workers, of mortgages, decaying cities and unemployment, only occasionally, for a few hours on those evenings when audiences gathered in theatres, hushed and waiting for the performance to begin.

At last the choreographer called a halt and reminded them of the next rehearsal time. Some of the dancers drifted away, bags in hand, presumably to change; others, Robert among them, came over to talk, the conversation soon drifting off into other matters, a performance someone had seen. It was obvious they all knew each other well; here Robert's voice was louder, more animated, as if this was where he came to life while with Mark he did little more than sleep, relax and dream. Mark watched the group, uncertain whether to stay where he was or to join in, aware that time was passing, that it would be too late for the film he and Robert had planned to see. He wanted to tell Robert he was bored, but did not know whether he had the right to do so, whether he could interrupt, how far into Robert's life he could intrude.

'I like it,' Robert said, looking around at the plump sofas and deep armchairs and the people, young and old, vivacious and detached, that filled them.

'Worth the effort?' Mark teased, remembering the disdain on Robert's face as he put on an old jacket and tie and stared at his reflection.

'Well,' he conceded, 'everyone should have tea at the Ritz at least once and if you have to dress up to do so. . .'

'And starve for the rest of the week.'

'You're paying.'

'It's my birthday,' Mark reminded him. 'That makes it more your responsibility.'

'I've already given you your present.' A framed photograph of himself, a solitary figure leaping across a darkened stage.

'And it was much appreciated. Wouldn't it be nice to be rich?' Mark went on, his eye caught by an elegantly and expensively dressed woman in her thirties.

'No,' said Robert. 'Too much money would distract me.'

'But if you were rich you wouldn't have to worry about getting a job. You could dance for yourself.'

'What would be the point? I need the edge, the point where people will pay me to dance but leave me the freedom to decide what to put on. If it's too egocentric they won't enjoy it and won't come; if it's too old-fashioned I'll be bored, it would only be a routine. I have to keep a balance. Money would destroy it.'

'If I were rich I could give up teaching. Concentrate on writing.'

'Would you? Or would you just sit around all day?'

Although his tone was softer, sometimes Robert's words reminded Mark of Gene. 'Maybe,' he said, to cut the conversation short. 'But it's all hypothetical.'

'When do you go back to the studio?' Robert asked after a pause.

'Tomorrow. It's the last time.'

'And then?'

'And then it's edited and I get the master and some copies.'

'It must be costing you.'

'It is.'

'But it's worth it.' Robert was confirming as much as asking.

'I think so. The guitarist yesterday asked me why I'd never made a recording before.' I don't know, Mark had answered; I didn't have the money, or the confidence.

'You must let me listen to it,' Robert said.

'I will, I will.'

His mouth moved lightly down Robert's neck and onto his chest; it reached the nipple and played with it, was about to suck it and the muscle beneath deeper within. 'Not tonight,' Robert whispered, gently pushing him away. 'No?' Mark asked, not quite believing what he had heard, unable to accept that after six days of waiting, six days of sleeping apart, six days of seeing each other for only twenty minutes or an hour at a time, that Robert might not want to make love.

'No.'

'Why not?'

'I'm exhausted. It's been a long week.'

'For me too.' It was difficult to keep the frustration, the recrimination out of his voice.

'But you don't use your body all the time, twelve hours a day. I just don't have the energy. Tomorrow? O.K.?' Robert sat up and kissed him, his lips no more than touching Mark's, a parent comforting a child, before he lay back again.

'O.K.' Mark said nothing more, certain that it was the truth and not an excuse, a rationale for dwindling interest and desire. Yet it left him discontented, wanting not only the physical release but the opportunity to express all the emotion which had to be suppressed during the week, which had no greater outlet than the casual touching of knees under a café table, arms resting on each other's thighs in the darkness of the cinema, a kiss disguised as a fraternal embrace. Even these were dissatisfying, made Mark – and, he was sure, Robert – feel like an uncertain teenager or a criminal passing drugs. So they touched in public less and less, building up an expectation which had now been belied. He wanted to resolve the situation but could not, for he would be satisfied neither by a solitary, sterile act in the bathroom nor by forcing Robert to stay awake, to take part in limited and begrudging sex. Irritated, disappointed, Mark turned over, wondered how long his ill-feeling would keep him awake and was soon, despite himself, asleep.

'You look tired.'

'I am.' Mark dropped into the chair opposite Robert.

'A hard day?'

'Yes! Teaching is tiring, believe it or not. What about you, what have you been doing?'

'Wandering around, looking at bookshops.'

'Buy anything?'

'These.' Robert passed a paper bag across the table.

'Hold on. Let me see what I want.'

'I've ordered tea.'

'You would. When the bomb has dropped and the world is collapsing around us, you'll be sitting calmly in some little place like this drinking tea.'

'Why not?' Robert asked. 'If I'm not dancing, it's the best way to go.'

Mark looked at the books – second-hand copies of Pirandello, Sartre, George Eliot. 'I don't know where you have the energy to get through these.'

'They're not difficult.'

'They're not difficult but they require concentration. Especially after a long day at school.'

'What were you doing?' The tea arrived. Robert checked its strength and poured out two cups.

'The last period was Ray Bradbury. It's fun for the kids; I don't mind it, but it's easy for them to get off the subject, which doesn't help me with their assessment.'

'Just pass them all.'

'If I could. But it's more difficult than that. I have to be able to justify the marks.'

'Well, never mind. By the end of the year you'll be out of it.'

'You seem to have more confidence in my abilities than I have.'

'That's not difficult.' Robert grinned.

'Fool!' Mark aimed an imaginary cushion. 'So you're enjoying your freedom.'

'One day is hardly freedom.'

'And tomorrow's your first night. What am I supposed to say?'

'Break a leg.'

'As long as that's all you break. I'm looking forward to it, you know.'

As in the rehearsal, when Robert danced it seemed that he was unaware of the audience and only partly aware of those around him, but when the curtain fell and he took his bow, a smile, self-confident but not proud, creased his face under the sweat that poured down from his brow and

Mark saw that he had been conscious throughout of his responsibility to himself, to his partners, to all the people who had given time and money to come and watch; only now, when it was over, could he relax and acknowledge what he had given them. He stepped back, joined hands with the rest of the cast to bring them forward and Mark saw his eyes searching the small auditorium, an expression of concern on his face sharper than Mark had ever seen. That's for me, Mark realised; he can't see me. For a moment he was tempted to thrust his hand in the air, to wave it wildly from side to side to catch Robert's attention, but their eyes crossed; he grinned and Robert's fear dissolved into the broadest of smiles. He needs me, Mark thought, feeling tears building up behind his eyes, he needs me. His gaze never leaving Robert, he clapped harder and harder.

It was strange to come back into the flat, to drop bags onto the kitchen table, to open the bedroom door gently and see Robert still sleeping. Mark would stare at the face with the slightly open mouth, the shoulder that sometimes jutted out from under the cover, the shapeless mound of the body, and it would seem that it was still the early morning, that the two or three hours Mark had spent quietly leaving the bed and the room, making himself tea and toast, going out to the supermarket and coming back with plastic bags full, were hours stolen out of time; if he undressed and got back into bed, it would still be only eight o'clock and the whole day would be ahead of them. Once or twice he had done that, but lifting the covers so that he could slide his cold body into the warmth had disturbed Robert, broken the spell and woken him, so that when Mark looked at the clock he saw that it was indeed half past eleven or noon; and by the time Robert was properly awake and they had perhaps made love, dressed and had something to eat, it was already early afternoon and their choices of how to spend their day were limited. So now he would look in and, once assured that Robert was still sleeping, but not so deeply that light sounds would not wake him, Mark would return to the kitchen, put away the shopping while water was boiling and toast was browning and take a tray with breakfast through to the lover who, like Sleeping Beauty, was about to be awoken with a kiss.

'What happened?'
'Nothing happened.'
'You didn't phone.' And Mark had spent an evening unable to concentrate, watching the most mindless comedies and games shows.
'I couldn't get away. The class went on too long.'
'You could've phoned afterwards.'
'It was too late. There was no point.'
'I thought something had happened to you.'
'Nothing happened.'
'Then why didn't you phone?'
'Because it was too late.'
This was circular, the argument returning to where it had started. Yet Mark somehow had to make Robert see how important the issue was. 'Look, this happened before.'
'And you made the same fuss about it.'
'It's not a fuss; it's important. If you say you're going to do something, do it.'
'But I can't always.'
'You could.'
Robert looked exasperated. 'Let's leave it,' he said. 'I'm sorry if it so upset you.' Slight sarcasm lay under his words.
'Don't be sorry; just don't do it again.' Mark was in the classroom, a teacher explaining to a dim and truculent child.
'I won't, if I can help it.'
You could help it last time, Mark thought, saying nothing.

The evening stretched behind him like the memory of a warm and reassuring dream. They had met as the pubs were opening, gone on to have a meal, see a film and return to the bar to sit and talk until it closed and it was

97

time for Robert to catch the last bus home. Their conversation had flowed as naturally as it always did, swept along by a deeper, wordless communication free of hesitation and confusion, each understanding immediately what the other was saying, the thoughts and implications behind words. As they stood by the bus stop, a little apart from the small crowd who waited peacefully, enjoying the day's lingering warmth, Mark tried again to persuade Robert to come home with him, countering every argument that Robert put up – I can lend you clean clothes, I can lend you money – without convincing him. The ritual, which in early days had been tense, was now good-humoured, for Mark had come to accept reluctantly that Robert needed time alone, needed to feel independent, that this separation was not a mute criticism of himself or their relationship. Yet, he allowed himself to imagine, if the bus that was now approaching from the distance had been Mark's train, if Robert had at last agreed that he would lose nothing by accompanying Mark home, the perfect evening that had just passed would have had the perfect ending. Instead he could only stand and watch the loudly joking and slightly drunk group jostle aboard and purse his lips discreetly as Robert took his turn at the end of the queue.

As Robert stepped up, he turned casually and said, 'There's something I forgot to tell you.'

'What?'

'I think I'm falling in love.' He turned away; the door closed behind him and the bus pulled off, as Mark stood, ecstatic and astounded, not sure if he could allow himself to believe what he had just heard.

IV

'I don't know how you put up with me,' Carl said, his hand resting on Mark's chest, his gaze directed down to some indeterminate point at the end of the bed.

98

'Now or then?'

'Then.'

'What else could I do?'

'You should've kicked me out.'

'How could I? I loved you.'

'And now?' Carl asked.

'I still love you.'

Their eyes met. They kissed for a moment.

'You made me see sense,' Carl went on.

'You would have seen it anyway.' It was easy to be magnaminous when you had won, when the weeks, months of discontent, argument and unhappiness, led to this new, stronger, beginning.

'No, I wouldn't. Thank you.' Carl reached over and kissed him again, long, deep, a kiss of love and affection, not passion.

'I did think about asking you to go,' Mark admitted. 'But I couldn't. I kept thinking either things'll get better or they'll get so bad you'll just leave. Then you got that job and I thought, well, let him settle into it, get a little money together – as if you'd ever save any money –'

'I'm learning.'

'-and then when you had enough money to go somewhere else I'd ask you to go. But by that time things had changed; it was working again.'

'Do you know why I took that job?'

'No. I still don't understand it. After all you used to say about never working in a pub. . .'

'Remember the day before we had that terrific argument about money and me and drinking?' The worst day, the day when Mark's anger and frustration had spilled out unchecked; he had made several comments he did not want to remember and had only been prevented by a perverse pride from voicing the hope that Carl would just leave and never come back. 'You were right, I knew, but I wasn't going to give you the pleasure of admitting it.' Carl grinned in apology. 'That was the night I went out and got pissed out of my head, deliberately, because it was going to be the last time. And the next morning I had a splitting headache, one of the worst hangovers I've ever had, but

I went out and got a job. I knew I'd get one – I'd always known I could get one. There's always a pub that's short of staff; all I had to do was go round three or four and ask.'

'I remember being surprised when I came home and found that note.'

'And you came round to see me.'

'Of course I came round. And saw you standing behind the bar as pleased as punch. You actually looked happy. I hadn't seen you happy in weeks.'

'I was happy. Even when I was doing the afternoon shift and my head was banging like someone's drum and my mouth tasted like a dustbin, I was happy. Something had happened – I don't know what – but it was just good to be there.'

'I didn't think it was going to last.'

'I knew it would. I just hoped you'd notice. I really wanted to please you; I really wanted to make up for all that had gone on. You know there were mornings, even after I got the job, when I thought he's going to tell me to go. And you didn't. That means something; it means a lot. I love you, Mark. I really love you.'

Mark saw the tears forming in Carl's eyes, felt both embarrassment and a sense of power. 'Forget it,' he said, leaning over and kissing him. 'It's in the past. What's important is here and now.'

Spots of paint were splashed across Carl, on his face, in his hair, over most of his clothes. It was non-drip, but spattered as Carl attacked the wall with enthusiasm. Mark followed him, covering the patches Carl had missed, smoothing over the thicker areas that threatened to harden into lumps. Together they worked fast and well; the gloomy brown room that was nominally Carl's but was seldom entered would soon be bright and colourful and the furniture that was cluttering the hall would be back and out of the way. Then there was only the hall itself to be painted, the last stage in obliterating the personality of the previous owner, an elderly spinster who had lived and probably died here. Mark's first few weeks after moving in had been spent carefully and patiently cleaning and decorating, but his interest had waned as he had first been engrossed by Carl's presence and later preoccupied with keeping Carl with him, keeping their relationship afloat. Now that that period had passed, like a heavy and frightening storm on a night at sea, he could turn his attention back to his flat and make all of it finally his home.

Yet it was as much Carl's home as his own, and the fact that it was Mark's name on the title and mortgage and Mark who received rent each week from his lover, offering him nothing more substantial than another seven days' shelter and warmth in return, disturbed him, suggested that Carl was no more than a kept boy who could be disposed of at short notice without recompense. The situation should be regulated, Carl offered a means of buying into the joint ownership which would give him security and still Mark's conscience. What held Mark back was the vague but real doubt that neither was ready for such a step, would yet commit himself to something as binding as marriage. It was as well to curb his impatience, to accept that a minor injustice now was better than a major entanglement in the unforeseen future. Meanwhile, they continued painting until Mark, seeing the figure he loved in front of him, the thick hair falling over the collar, the faded, torn shirt and the old and too tight jeans, could not resist putting his brush down, going over and kissing him.

'You used to sleep around a lot, didn't you?' Carl asked.

'Not really,' Mark said. 'Ten, fifteen people a year. That's not many. None since I met you.'

'You don't want to sleep with anyone else, do you?'

'There are one or two I wouldn't mind. . .' Truth indeed lay in jest.

'Don't. I couldn't stay with you if you did.'

There was a rare sharpness to Carl's tone. 'Why not?' Mark asked.

'I don't want to catch AIDS! I don't want *you* to catch it.'

'But of course I'd use a condom.'

'I still wouldn't stay. I'm not joking, Mark.'

'Why? Why do you feel so strongly about it? I wouldn't mind if you slept with someone else.' Was that true? He wouldn't want Carl to bring someone home, but nor did he want to tie Carl down, to see him as a possession over which he, Mark, held all control. 'I mean I wouldn't mind if you did it once or twice. If it got to be a habit I'd be worried.'

Carl shook his head. 'Don't worry about it. I wouldn't.'

'But why do you mind me doing it?'

'Because if I knew you'd slept with someone else it would make me feel dirty. You'd just be a tramp and I don't want to live with a tramp. I want to live with you.'

'So it's not just AIDS.'

'I don't want you to catch AIDS. I don't want to watch you die.'

'But it's not just AIDS.'

They were both silent. Carl sat watching as if daring Mark to challenge what he had always known but they had never discussed so clearly.

'Mark,' Carl said. 'Promise me you'll never sleep with anyone else.'

'Sleep, no. Have sex. . .' Carl's expression told him the humour was not appreciated. 'That's a lot to ask.'

'No, it isn't. I don't want to sleep around.'

But I do. Or I want the freedom to do so, even if I never take it up. Giving Carl what he wanted sounded like closing the prison door, locking himself in, throwing away the key. Or was the freedom false? A hangover from youth, when it was important to sow oats, to gain experience? If he loved Carl, if he was living with Carl, what was the point in having sex with others? He'd lose something if he didn't, a kind of thrill, excitement, but that was not much. And he'd guarantee himself an AIDS-free life. So it was a prison. But it wasn't solitary confinement; he would have Carl and Carl's presence would make the cell warmer, more comfortable and more secure than the freedom that Mark might otherwise miss.

Carl was still looking at him, the old expression of fear,

of worry that everything might be going wrong, lining his face. Of course Mark could not refuse him, did not want to refuse him, this or anything else. 'O.K.,' he said.

'You won't sleep around?' Carl was wary.

'No.'

'Not with anyone?'

'No.'

'You promise?'

'I promise.' Instead of the weight Mark had expected came a lightness, a sensation that he had not only glimpsed but ensured the future – a future that was bright, welcoming and beckoning. He looked across at Carl, saw his lover's relief and smiled.

The new term had started and most evenings Mark would return to an empty flat. Occasionally he was early and Carl would be there, would offer to make him tea and sometimes have a few minutes to drink it with him before he put on jacket and scarf, kissed him and left for work. Generally, however, Mark stayed at school to attend some meeting, finish correction or catch up on the assessments that were always demanding his time, and arrived back to a note on the table in the hall which told him what he expected and never asked for, that dinner was ready to be eaten or heated, and which always ended in some endearment which, however clichéd, made Mark smile, made him want Carl to be here so that he could hug and thank him.

He promised himself that he would go out some evenings, that he would catch up on the films or plays that Carl never wanted to see, but he seldom did, preferring to relax over his meal with the television or newspaper before going out to the pub where Carl worked. There he would sit by the bar and watch his lover serve and joke with the customers, see that here Carl had a more confident, outgoing personality than the one Mark was familiar with, and envy him his ability to get on with even those who were pompous, drunk or aggressive. Meanwhile Mark came to be recognised and accepted as Carl's 'friend' by the manager, his wife and the regulars, to be greeted and occasionally offered drinks, drawn into conversation and made the butt of good-humoured jokes. He responded politely, but was never totally at ease with these builders and salesmen, these brash young men and their fashionable girlfriends or their sometimes cynical, sometimes jovial parents, aware he had nothing in common with them and fearing that his distance was seen as condescension. At the end of the evening, therefore, he never regretted seeing the bar locked up, Carl give the counter a last wipe, put on his jacket and smile to say it was time to go home.

'I wanted to hurt you, you know.' Carl made the confession in the restaurant where Mark had taken them to celebrate the year they had been together. 'I didn't want you to love me.'

'Why not?' Mark asked. 'Why shouldn't I love you? Even though you made it bloody difficult at times.'

'I know.' Carl grinned apologetically. 'I didn't want you to get close. I wasn't going to stay.'

'What do you mean?'

'Do you remember I got a letter from Edwin?'

'Yes.'

'He told me he'd left the guy he was with. He wanted me to come back.'

The words made Mark curious but calm; whatever the threat was, it was over. 'And. . ?'

'I didn't know what to do. I was in love with you but I was also in love with Edwin. I'd come to London because he wouldn't sort himself out, then I got a letter saying he was living on his own and he wanted me to come home.'

'So why didn't you go?'

'Because I loved you!' In Carl's voice there was an echo of the anguish Mark had known.

'You should have told me, or just gone.'

'I couldn't. You would've been so upset.'

Yes, I would, Mark thought; it would have meant losing everything, going back to the beginning, being alone, going out to the bars, to the discos, standing in a crowd, wondering how tired I was going to be next morning, but not going home in case in the next five, ten, fifteen minutes the unknown guy I was waiting for, the one I was going to meet, who I was going to take home, who would take your place as you had taken Gene's, walked in looking for me as I was looking for him. 'Did you write to Edwin?'

'I phoned him.'

All this was happening and I never realised it. 'What did you tell him?'

Carl hesitated. 'That the same thing had happened to me as had happened to him. I was stuck in a relationship.'

'That you didn't like.'

'Don't say that!' Carl looked miserable, about to cry. 'I don't know what I thought. I just thought everything would be easier if you didn't like me, if I was a bastard. Then I could go back to Edwin and you'd find someone else. But I lost my job and I couldn't go home without any money.'

'Why not?'

'I don't know! Maybe I just wanted to stay. You were so good to me. You were so kind and patient and you loved me. And I didn't want to, but I loved you.'

Kind and patient; these were not words that Mark associated with himself. Yet, he realised, he had been kind and patient with Carl, had not thrown him out as others would have done. It was because he loved Carl and, he suddenly understood, love was a deeper and stronger force than he had ever imagined.

'There was something else,' Carl went on. 'I didn't know if I could trust you.'

'What do you mean?'

'I thought maybe you'd get bored. You'd say you loved me and after a couple of months you'd be after someone else.'

'I'm not like that,' Mark said.

'I know that now. I didn't then.'

They looked at each other, Mark seeing Carl as if all that he had just heard was dirt on a child's face that had been washed away, lines of age and worry that had been carefully erased. 'I didn't understand what was going on,' he said. 'You seemed to turn against me and I didn't know why.'

'Do you forgive me?'

'Don't be silly. There's nothing to forgive.'

'I love you more than ever,' Carl told him. 'I never want to leave you. You mean so much to me now.'

One year down. Ten, twenty, fifty to go.

Sometimes he felt paternal towards Carl, listened to him talk about the bar not because he was interested but because it gave Carl pleasure, watched trivial television programmes and helped him with competitions that he found in newspapers and on the backs of food packets for the same reason. Aware of Carl's lazy and undirected intelligence, he more than once suggested that he look for a better job, get some qualification in catering, but Carl shrugged such ideas aside, claimed that he was happy where he was, that he didn't need to be his own boss, that he'd be bored by college and study. Maybe in a year or two, but not now; he was happy with the routine, did not mind the low pay, saw his earlier insistence on working in nightclubs as a snobbery that he'd put behind him. Underlying this lack of ambition Mark saw, and was made slightly uneasy by, the fact that Carl was happy, that living with and housekeeping for Mark was enough for him, that he did not want anything more.

Although they seldom had free time together, it was then that they would visit or invite friends, in whose company their different needs coincided. Carl enjoyed having people around him, liked to be part of a group that was talking, drinking and laughing while Mark appreciated being able to relax, to let himself go in a way that he could not at school and did not want to with Carl. He was happy to see his lover happy, and happy to spend an evening or a Sunday afternoon playing mindless games or exchanging harmless gossip. That friends did not have to be debating partners, grindstones on which to sharpen one's view of the world, came as a mild surprise to Mark; such an attitude, he realised, being a hangover from university days. That same had to be true of a lover, that the affection and companionship which came from living with someone easily compensated for the often nerve-wracking intensity that was a component of the dizzy sensation of falling in love. Just being with Carl was pleasurable and for that pleasure Mark was grateful.

Mark might be frustrated on Carl's behalf, might want him to better himself, make himself more of Mark's equal and less of his houseboy, but that emotion seldom appeared. It would indeed be nice if they had more in common, if Carl overcame his petty prejudices and allowed himself to be taken to the theatre or cinema, if he were even more critical, nagged Mark into making his tape and hawking it round producers. But these were secondary thoughts, undercurrents that seldom disturbed the flow of good feeling that now dominated Mark from the moment he woke up to each night when, whether or not they made love, they curled into one another in the warmth of the bed.

'Guess what I just heard.' Carl rejoined Mark where he was lounging at the bar.

'What?'

'You see those two guys over by the telephone?'

Mark looked out of the corner of his eye at the twenty or so men who had gathered in this gay pub early in the evening. 'One with a moustache and the other in a leather jacket?'

'Yes.'

'What about them?'

'When I was coming out of the gents I heard the one in the jacket say that that guy at the bar had a beautiful arse.'

'Meaning me?'

'Yes, dumbskull, you.'

Mark straightened up, not so much from embarrassment as self-consciousness. Involuntarily he glanced back at the two men and caught the eye of the one who had complimented him. 'He's quite attractive,' he said, seeing the expression of amusement in a young and friendly face.

'I prefer the other one,' Carl said without turning.

'Shall we pair off?'

'I hope you're joking. Sometimes I don't know if you are.'

Sometimes, Mark thought, neither do I.

It was half an hour before they left the bar to meet friends of Carl's who were spending a few days in London. Half an hour in which Mark talked to his lover as he had always done and half an hour in which he guardedly looked over at the young man watching him with growing interest. He was Carl's age but taller, had short black hair that was trained back and up to emphasise a smooth and neat face; his body was slim, the jacket either emphasising or creating broad shoulders and suggesting muscular arms. He looked like someone who enjoyed life, who was more interested in action than in consequences. His presence and gaze challenged Mark, challenged him to leave Carl, to find an excuse to get away for an hour, to meet him and . . . and make love. Disturbed by an emotion and hunger that he had thought dead and forgotten, Mark walked out with his lover into the cold autumn street, glancing back as he did so to confirm that the stranger's eyes were still on him, that they were still offering what Mark wanted but could not have.

THREE

His capacity for sleep surprised him. He had thought he would spend hours shifting and turning, his body on its back, its side, its front, his limbs crooked or straight, hugging himself or sprawled over the edge, each position reflecting a different thought, a different emotion, Robert's idea of him, his own anger at being misunderstood or regret at having caused them both pain. Instead, he had fallen asleep easily, as if his mind, overworked and exhausted from having gone over every nuance of Friday's conversation many times, had rebelled and refused to consider any matter other than its own rest and well-being. So, after a deep sleep which ended in a vivid dream of an exotic city where he walked and ran through empty, glittering streets in search of some wonderful, unknown treasure, he woke to the luxury of a Sunday morning and a day in which there was nothing to do and everything that could be done.

He dozed until the bed's comfort and warmth lost its attraction and got up to find that he was alone in the flat. Wherever Ben had gone – whether visiting one of the many friends and acquaintances whose names Mark knew but whose faces he had never seen, or playing some sport with the same energy and efficiency as he approached every activity – Mark appreciated the solitude, was grateful for the freedom to play the radio loudly, to sprawl across the kitchen, to be clothes-less or semi-nude. It was a freedom he would not lose if Robert lived here. . . His thoughts began but were stifled before they could dominate him as they had the day before.

The day was warm, but clouds littered the sky and Mark

felt no urge to go out. He was content to let time pass as he had previously planned, perhaps cleaning, watching an old film if one were scheduled, writing the song which was already, unbidden and unsupervised, forming itself in his mind. First, however, there would be breakfast, the luxury of eggs and bacon, of toast and marmalade, a full pot of coffee that would last through the day and the thick Sunday newspaper that lay invitingly on the table where Ben had put it down. Yet it was not long before the reports of political intrigue and violence at home and wars and developments abroad lost their interest, appeared as no more than the neuroses of insecure individuals writ irritatingly large, while the pages of fashion, gossip and travel appealed to a snobbery that he did not at that moment share. In search of entertainment he turned to the crossword, but after two or three clues pushed it aside and found himself staring at the heavy branches that bobbed slowly outside his window. They reminded him of the occasions, frequent as a child, rare as an adult, when he lay on grass under trees and saw above him the green leaves swirling against a blue background as a different country, one that was not physical but emotional, one that, like a glimpse of paradise granted to the damned, could be observed but never entered. That was the feeling, the illusion, indescribable and ineffable, which he always wanted and always failed to infuse into his songs.

'Late again, rain again, time to go home.' No, the image was too mournful, too depressing, while the rhyme and words were merely trite. Besides, in the story that was waiting to be put down there was no rain – it was a bright windy day and the woman (Why a woman? Why did so many of his songs feature women?) who had come to meet her lover would wait for him, would not go home, would, as she accepted that he would not come, could not come, find consolation in the park, in the wind, in the trees. Perhaps the trees themselves bore her away; perhaps she changed, became one of them, became the wind. And the music that accompanied her, that described her, described the park as clearly as did the lyrics, would be steady, firm, with a recurring phrase for the wind and trees and an echo or vibrato to convey the other-worldliness that would grow more dominant as the song progressed, would fuse with the words towards the end in a sense of wonder, a sense of joy.

The idea was good, but so were all his ideas before he wrote them down, nailed them to the page with syllables and notes that preserved their form, yet, no matter how much care he took, however gentle he was, drained them of life. Perhaps today, with the strength and confidence that was surging up within him again, like a river that has flowed underground for miles and suddenly reappears, he would succeed, would find at last his ability equal to his ambition. If that were the case, he would soon know. Not immediately – he did not yet feel strongly enough about this particular song, did not feel it clamour for his attention, insist on being given life and form – but soon, in no more than a few hours.

He stood up, gathered together the dishes and left them in the sink for the moment when he would welcome the opportunity of short, mindless activity. What he wanted now was a bath, to let its warmth settle round him and his thoughts wander where they will. He ran the water and pulled off his clothes slowly, wishing that it was Robert's hands undoing the buttons and easing off the sleeves and trouser legs as he wished the water he slid into was Robert's embrace, his kiss. He wondered where Robert was now, how the first performance had gone, where the company had spent the night, whether they had to rehearse again or had the morning free. He found himself thinking about Robert with as much curiosity but less urgency than had occupied him the day before and, searching for the anger of the previous week and yesterday's fear that had supplanted it, he was surprised to find little more than benevolent indifference. No, his feelings were not so neutral, so unconcerned, but this morning he was no longer obsessed with his lover, no longer afraid that his taking back the tape and his attempts to justify that action had been misunderstood. And if that fear had gone, dissipated like a fever in his sleep, what had taken its place was not another fear, another obsession, but calm, an awareness that whatever was to happen between them, whether their next meeting was cold or wary or as warm as before, had already been decided and there was nothing he could do about it, no way he could or should influence what Robert felt.

With the relief and light-heartedness of a burden removed, an obligation cancelled, Mark sank under the water, seeking there a deeper peace until the pressure of his lungs forced him to sit up and gasp for breath. The water swirled around him, eddied and flowed; it was, if not itself a caress, then its substitute, its echo. A month ago he had indeed been caressed in this bath, not by Robert but by a boy who had briefly taken Robert's place, who, as if the light were weak or the perspective somehow changed, had momentarily appeared to Mark as another lover. The episode had been both intriguing and satisfying and one which Mark knew, with neither regret nor guilt, might easily happen again.

It had been the middle of the week, another evening enjoyably spent and brought to an artificial close by the bus which sucked Robert in and drove him away. Mark's irritation that once again he had failed to persuade Robert to spend the night with him was compounded by the fact that it had been three days since he had had any form of sexual release. The thought of masturbating, of substituting his own mechanical action for the warmth and presence of another body, fuelled his mood rather than assuaged it; it was self-righteously, telling himself that if Robert had been with him he would not have been forced into such a situation, that he walked not towards the tube station but the nearest gay disco. There he might meet no one, might find himself in the early morning arriving home tired and alone, but at least he would have made the effort, would have acknowledged his needs rather than swept them aside yet again. As for Robert, there could be no recrimination; a relationship that had its foundations in adultery and found its strength in mutual respect could hardly impose, had never tried to impose, a hypocritical and ultimately suffocating morality.

Andy had stood on the edge of the dance-floor, a

112

slim figure in anonymous jeans and white shirt who returned Mark's look without encouraging it. Robert's age, he looked and acted no older than he was and it was this uncertainty, this lack of assurance which drew Mark, the impression of someone old enough to know how to behave in bed and not so old as to have unalterable ideas as to what should happen there. Mark approached him, prepared for rejection, and was greeted with shy curiosity, an acceptance of his offer to dance and, ten minutes later, of the drink that would cement their brief relationship. Sitting in a quiet corner, Mark probed his new partner with tact, unwilling, he later realised, merely to have sex, wanting this encounter as he wanted every encounter to be more than merely sex, to be at the very least an exchange of affection, a meeting of even vaguely sympathetic minds. He learned therefore, and the information was infused by the latent promise of intimacy with a romance much greater than the words, that Andy was a trainee chef, a newcomer to London from some East Anglian town, who frequented bar and disco less from eagerness to dance and drink than from a lack of alternatives to evening solitude. Although no extrovert, he proved to be less timid than he had at first appeared; and Mark discovered with a growing sense of excitement that his desire was not diminishing as it sometimes did with others when the optimism of his imagination had to yield to mundane reality.

The invitation to go home together was easily offered and easily accepted. Too impatient to wait for the night bus and reluctant to allow Andy time to hesitate, to reconsider, Mark hailed the first taxi they saw. As it drove them across Westminster Bridge he thought briefly about Robert, but the image that flickered through his mind was no more substantial than that on a television screen, one that faded abruptly as Andy asked him how far they had to go. Thirty minutes later, in the bedroom, he found himself hugged and fiercely kissed, the opening move in a rite intensified by Mark's hunger for muscles and skin rather than words and mind and by Andy's hunger for arms to embrace him and a body to be embraced.

Their love-making was tender rather than aggressive; and Mark found himself staring down at the thin, pale body half-wondering in what way he could hold it, kiss it, give it strength and flesh, character and colour. Afterwards, when they lay back, arranged the covers and settled into positions in which each could fall comfortably asleep, Andy was not silent but in the mood to talk, to ask how long Mark had lived here, whether he was alone, whether he had a lover. To the last question Mark was evasive, concerned that he had betrayed not Robert but Andy, for it was clear from Andy's words and tone, from the way his hand held Mark's and their bodies curved into each other that he considered the last hour had been only the first stage of a relationship, had signalled as clearly as a guard's whistle or an alarm the end of the loneliness he carefully but unsuccessfully disguised. As he gave his vague answer Mark recognised, in outline rather than detail, the diffident teenager he himself had once been, the same uncertain manner and the same deep-rooted if unstated belief that given time, patience and enough searching the ideal lover would appear. The nine years that separated them were as wide as any generation gap; he had, unwittingly and almost unwillingly, gained an experience and outlook far beyond that of the youth now lying beside him and hesitantly offering his love and friendship. To realise that someone else could be so young was an unwelcome intimation that he himself was growing old, that age, even when unbeckoned, still approached. He reached down and kissed Andy's brow, a father, an elder brother, protecting, loving, blessing the younger son.

They woke early the next morning, Andy's arm firmly round Mark, their feet entangled at the edge of the bed and warmth between them like a fat and sleepy cat. As they bathed together and wiped each other down, the intensity of Andy's stare and presence so flattered and disturbed Mark that he briefly wondered if both could call in sick, could free the day to be alone to get to know each other, to see if the unspoken promise could be fulfilled. Andy, however, had to leave. He asked at the door if they could

114

meet again and, when Mark agreed, promised to phone the next day. Mark, turning back to the empty flat, to the extra cup of tea he had time to drink, thought back over the last few hours, remembered with a start Robert, and asked himself whether he could, whether he wanted to have two lovers in his life. But the new emotion died as easily as it had been born, stifled by the memory of Robert and the realisation that his attention could never be equally and fairly divided. When Andy called and Mark heard the naivety, the traces of effeminacy, the eagerness to please that he had earlier ignored, he prevaricated, claimed he was busy for the next few days and would ring back. The disappointment he heard before replacing the receiver made audible his guilt that he had merely used Andy to satisfy his own physical greed while ignoring the boy's deeper and more important needs. He wanted to atone for his mistake, but to call back, to offer friendship in place of today's disinterest or yesterday's love was beyond his abilities and would, if badly handled, be more painful to Andy than the emotional bruises he had already received.

When Robert heard about Andy he reacted no more than if he had been told what film Mark had seen or which friend he had met. Mark was relieved, glad to have confirmed that he need not be ashamed, that a trivial incident did not have to be denied as if it were theft or murder, yet also disappointed that Robert did not offer even the mildest complaint or indication that he was offended, that he would have preferred the event not to have occurred. The reproof would have been welcome, evidence of Robert's feelings corroborating his presence, his conversation, his smile. Still, no reaction was better than Carl's reaction, his hostility to even the most tentative of Mark's remarks. At Christmas they had talked about going away, taking the holiday that they had never had. Italy, Mark had suggested, in the middle of summer, when the weather was hot and they both had money for a month or more away. Carl would be happy to go anywhere, insisted only that there be sun all day, a café to drink in and a beach nearby. 'But you'll do some sightseeing with me?' Mark asked, part insisting, part pleading.

'Sure,' Carl responded with neither enthusiasm nor distaste.

'An hour in a museum followed by an hour in a café watching the world – and the men – go by.'

'As long as you don't try to pick them up.'

'Why not?' Mark was irritated by the warning in Carl's tone. 'We'll be on holiday, abroad; what does it matter if one of us goes off for half an hour?'

'I won't.'

'You can if you want. I won't stop you. So why can't I?'

'You promised.'

'I know I promised. But what harm would it do if I had sex, half an hour's fun, with someone I'd never ever see again?'

'Who'd give you AIDS, which you'd then give to me. No thank you.'

'Not everyone has AIDS, Carl.' Mark heard and hated the whine in his voice. 'And I wouldn't do anything that wasn't safe.'

'Then go off and do it.' Carl's patience snapped. 'Go and sleep with whoever you want, do what you want, but don't come back to me. Go on, now. Be a whore, slut around if that's what you really want to do. And if that's all I or anyone else means to you I don't want to live with you. I don't want to be with you, I don't want to touch you.' He stared at Mark, the anger in his eyes, in the tautness of his face, as hard, as painful as a blow. 'Can't you see you're worth more than that, much, much more? You're wonderful, Mark, you're the best thing that's ever happened to me. Don't make yourself cheap – don't make *me* cheap – by running after every pretty boy you see.'

Mark heard the anguish, saw the frustration, came over to sit by Carl, to put a hand on his knee. 'I made a promise,' he said. 'I'll keep it. I just want to understand why it's so important to you, why it upsets you.' And if I know why, maybe I can chip away at your obstinacy, mould it, soften your way of thinking so you allow me my weakness, my occasional moments in someone else's bed.

116

'You always want to ask. You always want to talk, talk, talk, have everything explained. Do you have to?' Carl complained. 'Isn't it enough that I don't want you to sleep around? Can't you do that one thing for me?'

'Of course I can,' Mark said, aware that he was leaning, weighing down, treading on thin ice. 'But I'm curious, I want to know why you don't want me to.'

'I've seen too many people do it, too many marriages break up. It doesn't work. You can't say it doesn't mean anything, that it's just a game, because it isn't. Someone always gets hurt.'

Especially the children. Mark did not need to hear confirmed what he already knew, what he had learned from Carl's occasional comments, from the times when, in more relaxed mood, he talked about his family, his father and his father's second wife and his father's many mistresses, his mother, living alone and drinking to fuel her resentment of her fate and the world, Carl himself and his brothers, their difficult, sometimes angry, sometimes withdrawn childhoods and adolescences. No, there was no mystery for Mark to probe, no problem that prolonged questioning would solve. Mark understood well enough Carl's fear of adultery; what he did not understand was his own growing itch, his growing awareness of the good-looking young men who lived just beyond the world he lived in, who, each time his eyes caught theirs, seemed to beckon him, tantalise him, invite him to approach them. Nor could Mark understand why the freedom he had seemed to gain months ago with his promise to be faithful had imperceptibly dwindled to the claustrophobia of a comfortable but nonetheless restrictive prison. His love for Carl had not changed, was still the focus of his life – although it would never dominate them both as Carl's love for him sometimes seemed to do – but it no longer satisfied him, at times demanded more than it offered.

The prison gates had finally opened and Mark had been thrown back into the cold, exhilarating world. Now, months later, he sat at the piano trying to create another person's life, her search for love. He set down the words

117

first as he always did, with the notes clamouring impatiently at the edges of his mind, their presence forcing him to alter a phrase here, change an emphasis there. 'You follow the path beneath the trees, a woman alone in search of. . .' Love? No, he wanted to suggest the emotion, not hammer it home as did every pop song. Anyway, that whole phrase should come later, should follow an introduction that suggested a cool day, a spring breeze, the woman's strength and solitude. 'One May afternoon in an empty park, the city's noise dying in the wind.' That was better, closer to what he wanted to say.

He worked on, building words into phrases which he shifted backwards and forwards until he had created the body of a poem which, if not a magic formula to transform into sound every nuance of feeling he wanted to convey, at least began the process, pointed thoughts where he wanted them to go. When he was satisfied he sang the song a couple of times under his breath, his fingers lightly touching the keyboard, picking out the backbone of the tune. At last he stood up, stretched the curve out of his spine and looked down at what he had created as if the extra distance allowed him to see it more critically, more dispassionately. It was good, he knew, and with the satisfaction of a job well done he allowed himself time to go away and rest.

In the past, not that long ago, there had been days, weeks, when he had been unable to believe in himself, to believe that he could put words and music together that would entertain, fascinate, even educate people. Doubts had gnawed in him like the cravings of an addiction which could only be satisfied by destructively strong doses, not of a drug but of others' support and approval. At its worst, that craving for reassurance had made Mark its puppet, its mouthpiece, forced him to attack, attach himself to Gene in a night of despair and one-sided argument which had finally and irrevocably instilled in Mark a sense of his own abilities – at the cost of losing the lover he so much wanted.

They had left the restaurant sometime after midnight,

the warm and benevolent mood engendered by wine and each other's company having brushed aside Gene's brief moment of anger. It was too early to go home and Gene suggested that they walk across town to a bar that he knew. As they crossed the Seine it seemed to Mark that the city was different, that at some point in the evening, without his being aware of it, he had, as in an old science fiction story, crossed into another plane of existence, one which superficially resembled the world he had left, but which was in some way sharper, made foreign by the intensity of its shadows and the acuteness of its angles. Most alien and most welcome were the new emotions he was experiencing, as if until now his mind had seen in monotone and had suddenly been granted the gift of colour. People seemed different and Mark was certain that if he were to go up and speak to the few strangers they were passing, they would respond in ways that he would only dimly understand. Gene was the only familiar reference in this new world, and Mark looked on him with the same excitement and resentment of dependence as he would a guide who was leading him into the distant heart of a tropical jungle.

A dark door in a quiet narrow street opened to a cramped lobby and a pretty youth with an expression of boredom who took their entrance fee. A further door let them into a large room where, after a moment to focus through the haze of cigarette smoke and his own excitement, Mark saw men sitting back in comfortable chairs or leaning against the wall like models, like actors on stage waiting for the play to begin, each offering an attraction, their smooth beauty, their bright clothes or their smiles of experience. Between them floated women – or so their dress declared – as grandiose as matriarchs, as madams. Here and there were knots of conversation, of romance, of laughter, and hovering over all were the beat and voice of a dance record he did not recognise. In the middle of this room, this nightclub, this brothel, stood a horseshoe bar with two stools free for Gene and Mark to sit and a bartender to wait on them whose youth and confidence were as integral to him as his short, black and perfectly cut hair and smooth high cheeks. As they waited for their drinks, Mark wondered if Gene too found the boy attractive, whether the three of them could go back to the flat together, make love in an endless tangle of mouths and cocks and limbs, but the thought was too daring and the night too early for such a possibility to be seriously considered.

'I like this place,' he told Gene, after looking round at the warm if murky colours and up at the high and intricate ceiling.

'So do I, but I have to be in the mood.'

'Is this all of it?'

'There's a disco down there.' Gene pointed to the broad stairwell in the corner of the room. 'It's usually pretty crowded.'

'And upstairs?' Mark asked, seeing a figure descend as overdressed and as confident as Barbra Streisand in a period film.

'I'm not sure. Rest-rooms, maybe. Or I think it's where you put on your drag.'

'What do you usually wear?'

'Just a little off-the-shoulder number in black with the skirt slit to the hip.'

'And a long cigarette holder and a handbag?'

'No, a small terrier. He drinks martinis and growls at anyone he doesn't like. All the men fall in love with me but they're frightened to death of him. He's a terrific judge of character, saves mah poah virgin bahdy fram men who jist wahnt ta abuse me.'

'I can see there are depths to you I have yet to discover.' Mark could indeed see Gene as an androgynous figure in satin and found the picture both bizarre and seductive.

'Yes, I'm profound.' Gene spoke with a surprising sarcasm.

'Certainly more than I am. I can't think of things like that.'

'Like what?'

'Like your drag outfit.'

'What do you mean?'

'I mean I'm not imaginative. I'm not creative.'

120

'Mark, we went through this in the restaurant.'

'That was song-writing. This is something else.'

Gene was silent, his eyes on a corner of the room where a group of elegantly dressed young men and women lounged round a bottle of wine.

'Look at the people here. They've all got something I don't have, looks, style, self-confidence. What do I have? Nothing. Even the barman,' Mark turned, saw the youth lean over to take a customer's order, to receive, it appeared, a compliment, an invitation, a kiss. 'Even he's got more poise, personality, whatever you call it, than I'll ever have.' Mark's fist jerked in the air, looking for a table to hit, a desk to thump.

Gene followed Mark's gaze. 'He's just a pretty boy.'

'That's something, isn't it?'

'Oh, Mark.' Gene looked at him with an expression that could have been boredom or pity.

'What makes me special? Nothing. Nothing at all. I teach in a crummy school nine to five and that's it. That's me, Mark Robertson, teacher, failure.'

'What's wrong with being a teacher?'

'Is that what you want to be? Or a clerk?' Mark felt he was hitting a punch-bag that built up his anger by offering no resistance. 'Would you want to sit in an office for the rest of your life, live in some nice little flat in Chicago and have four weeks holiday in Mexico or in Europe every year? Of course not. But I have to. That's what I'm stuck with. That fucking school and little holidays to Paris when I can afford it. The only thing I have to be grateful for is I'm not unemployed.'

'You've got your songs.'

'I don't *know* that I have.' Again Mark wanted to hit something, to pound his point home. He waited for a moment, but the confirmation that he was seeking did not come. 'You've told me I'm a good song-writer and that we all have worries and uncertainties, but with me it's worse than that. It goes deeper. There's a great hole in the middle of me where my personality should be, which should give me strength, creativity, whatever the magic component is, but doesn't. I'm hollow, empty.'

Mark stopped, suddenly aware that he had talked himself into a labyrinth, into a new, unexplored and potentially self-destructive discussion.

'If that's how you feel. . .'

It was reassurance not dismissal that Mark wanted, needed to trick out of Gene. 'It's not how I want to feel. But I don't see any alternative.' Except you telling me everything's all right, shaking me, doing whatever it is you can to convince me that yes, I can write, yes, I have personality, yes, I am worth as much if not more than each of these people around us. But Gene said nothing and that silence not only hurt Mark but angered him, insulted him. If Gene had any feelings for Mark, had any feelings for the person who again and again had interrupted his own life and come this far, spent so much time and money to be with him, then he, Gene, owed it to Mark to bolster his confidence, to throw him a life-line, not to leave him floundering in a sea of doubts and fear. If Mark was entitled to anything from Gene, he was entitled at least to the semblance of allegiance and support. 'Don't you understand?'

'Yes, I do,' Gene replied, a concern in his voice that Mark had not noticed before.

'And?'

'And what?'

Mark looked at him, exasperated.

'Mark, you want something from me and I don't know what it is. I can't help you. I can't publish your songs for you. I can't sing them. I can't pay for you to give up your job and write. You've got to do all that yourself.'

'I can't,' Mark wailed.

'Then forget it. Accept you'll never be a song-writer.'

As if in a maze where every path led back to the same dead end, they had returned to the logical conclusion of Mark's argument. But, if only because every sign pointed in the direction that he did not want to go, a rare determination persuaded him that he not only could but would succeed, would, if only to persuade Gene that he was wrong, become famous, be respected for his songs. He looked round him and saw that he was not merely

122

surrounded by colour and talent and life but was part of it, belonged here, in this world, as much as the barman, the stout drag queen who was walking past and the man in leather who lounged arrogantly and incongruously against the far wall.

They sat in silence for a time. Mark stared at his empty glass, aware he was slightly and happily drunk. 'Shall we dance?' he suggested.

'I'm not in the mood.'

'Another drink?' Mark leaned forward to catch the barman's eye.

'No, I think I'll go home.'

The words were a shock which destroyed Mark's confidence as suddenly as it had returned.

'Why? We've only just got here.'

'I'm tired. You stay if you want.'

'Is it what I've been saying? I've stopped; I'm O.K. I've worked things out. Forget it. We'll talk about something else.'

'It's nothing to do with that,' Gene said. 'I just want to go home. It's the wine, the day . . . I don't know.'

What have I done? Why can I see everything crumbling? Why can't I do anything about it? I've failed; he's lost interest, his sleep's more important.

'Stay,' Gene repeated. 'You've got a key.'

'I don't want to stay.' Not if you aren't staying with me. 'I didn't come to Paris to sit on my own in a bar.' To look for a pick-up when my lover leaves me.

Gene drained his glass and stood up. With a feeling of helplessness, of loss, Mark followed him in silence towards the door. If there were only some way he could stop Gene, some magic word or phrase that would have him stop, turn round, smile, say let's dance, everything's O.K., I want you, I need you; but first the inner then the outer door opened before them and Mark found himself out in the dark, quiet, narrow street, the colour and hubbub continuing behind him as it drained from his thoughts, from his life.

It was a sensation that no longer repeated itself; since

Gene colour and confidence, shaky though the latter sometimes was, had become part of him, as permanent a feature as greying hair or a flattering beard. Perhaps, Mark thought as he poured himself more coffee and wandered back to the living-room, drawn to his song like an iron filing to a magnet, that night, although it still had many hours to run, had indeed seen him move onto another plane of existence, for, once he had recovered from the pain of leaving Gene, his life, his outlook had never seemed quite so gloomy, so hopeless, again.

He read the words in front of him over again. Already they sounded weaker, in places inadequate or immature, but it was always the case that he was soon disappointed by what he had written, that it would be several months before he finally decided whether the song was good or no more than competent. Besides, lyrics only outlined by music were naked – a cold, shivering body that had to be wrapped up, clothed in the sound of piano or guitar. When the melody was on the page, the tramlines' progress measured by bars in which the black and white notes sat like blinking eyes, all would be ready for his singing to bring this woman to life, to follow her through this serene and gently haunted park, to give voice to her thoughts, her wondering where her lover was, her wondering how much she knew him, how much she was loved.

The same question – how much he was loved – had occupied Mark's thoughts the evening, less than two weeks ago, that Robert had stepped away from him and, with his parting words, left Mark in a state of happiness and confusion. He had stood at the stop until the bus's warm light had dwindled and merged into the oranges and pale whites which stretched along Tottenham Court Road, then turned and walked automatically to the station to catch the tube, absently surveying middle-aged theatre-goers returning home alongside mildly drunk young women and their boyfriends. Not only had someone once again, willingly and unprompted, told him he was loved, but the occasional unsettling suspicions that Robert was losing interest, was getting bored, had been suddenly dismissed, were proved to be no more than whispers from the ghosts of his insecurity, his paranoia. Yet Mark could not help asking himself, if Robert truly loved him, why had he insisted that night as on every weekday night on going home, why did he not want to be with Mark, to celebrate, to make love and not just to state it? It was a riddle that Mark could worry over but not solve, like the telephone calls Robert would forget to make, the days, admittedly rare, that he was expected and did not appear, events – non-events – which, until now had repeatedly suggested to Mark that their brief romance was dying, had already died, that Robert was getting bored, was losing interest, had met someone more attractive, better read, more amusing, as infatuated with dance. All it had taken was one statement, a few words, and Mark had to rearrange his emotions yet again.

As the train approached his stop, Mark's thoughts reached out across London to the unknown territory of N10 where Robert, without ever giving Mark his full address, had admitted to living. He saw his lover (now he could use the word!) walking through suburban avenues to the home that Mark's imagination had built up from comments Robert dropped like unnoticed litter; a mock-Tudor semi-detached house where Robert's room was an oasis of books, posters and clutter in a desert of floral wallpaper; pink bathroom suite, a cocktail bar in the lounge. His mother would already be in bed – a Julie Walters of a woman, bright, uncertain, successfully fending off approaching middle age with energy and money – and hearing him come in, would want to call to him but be afraid that the gesture was too protective, would make of him a mummy's boy. And if she did call out or he knocked at the door and looked in, what would he say? 'Mum, I've had a great evening and I'm in love with a wonderful guy.' Or if he went straight to bed, would he be thinking about Mark, would he lie there into the early hours, unable to sleep for thinking about the man he loved?

Mark laughed to himself. He had no more idea of Robert's home life than, if he were honest with himself, of what most of the time was going through Robert's head.

The boy was only nineteen, and saw life very differently from Mark. So there were nights when he preferred to go home, days when he was held up by class or rehearsal – none of that implied criticism of his lover, a reluctance to be with him. Hadn't Mark himself seen Robert's wish to be alone as a sign of his independence, a welcome change from Carl's need always to be with him? Damn it, Robert had just proved how important Mark was to him and all he had done was stand on the pavement, mouth open like a gaping fish, like an autistic child. He had said nothing, not even offered a banality like 'thank you' or 'that's wonderful;' words which, if not as responsive as leaping onto the bus to kiss him or hauling him off for the same purpose or shouting out 'I love you too' so loudly that everyone aboard would turn and stare, would at least have shown Robert he cared, that he had heard what Robert had said.

You're an idiot, he told himself as the train pulled into his station. I'm going to phone him now and damn the hour and damn his mother and if she answers I'm going to say, 'Mrs Oliver, you have a wonderful son'. In under five minutes he had run home, walking up the stairs slowly to let his breath return so that he might calmly tell Robert what he had not had the wit or courage to tell him before. He dialled the number, heard the phone ring twice before Robert answered. Mark was held by a sudden and familiar nervousness but that did not prevent him from saying quietly, 'I know I'm in love with you'. They talked briefly and Mark went to bed in a state of excitement, certain that he would lie awake all night thinking about Robert, about himself, making plans, decisions, reorganising their lives so that when morning came the power of thought would have already transformed him into a successful performer and Robert into a dancer whose fame spread far beyond the stage. The animation, the enthusiasm did not last, however, and he soon fell asleep, waking hours later to a day where little of substance seemed to have changed.

The one night in his life he had not been able to sleep had been the night he had most needed to. Walking back with Gene from the nightclub, he had tried to make conversation, to recall the humour of his last visit, to do anything to erase the last three hours, cancel the admissions of inability and insecurity and win back Gene's respect. But to each comment of Mark's Gene had responded absently and Mark had trotted along like a punished child keeping up with his father, a dog whose master has more important things on his mind.

Silence accompanied them up the steep narrow stairs and into the small apartment. 'Do you want coffee?' Mark offered.

'No,' Gene said. 'I'm going to bed.'

'Then I'll come with you.' They undressed and Mark followed Gene between the blankets and the mattress on the floor, a reminder of the bohemianism to which he still sometimes aspired. As much consciously as automatically, a last attempt to restore the affection between them, Mark put his arm round Gene to draw them together, to bring his mouth into Gene's neck, where, a young animal on familiar territory, it nuzzled and kissed.

He was momentarily aware of the tension before he heard Gene say, his words vibrating through Mark's mouth as it paused on his skin, 'No, Mark, not now.'

'Why not?' He might as well ask, although he already knew.

'It's not the right moment.'

'It's because of this evening, isn't it?'

Mark felt the slight movement of Gene's sigh. 'No, Mark, it isn't. I'm. . .'

'What?'

'I just need to be left alone.'

'You want me to leave the bed?'

'No.'

'But you don't want me to make love with you.'

'Mark. . .' The note of warning in the father's voice.

He was about to speak, but realised that nothing he could say would bring Gene back, would bring him closer. He lay still for a time, staring up at the ceiling, at the cracks and stains just visible in the street-light that filtered in through the faint curtain. If he turned his head

127

he could see Gene's easel, his paintings and photographs on the walls, the battered couch at the far end of the room and the cups on the floor where they had been left after the coffee drunk that afternoon. Everything was still, the silence punctuated rarely by the passing of footsteps, of voices, discussions and arguments in a French that he only began to understand as it was dying away. Beside him lay Gene, motionless, a long, slim, desirable body and a mind equal to, superior than, his own. This was where Mark desperately wanted to be, this was where he wanted to live, this was what he was unworthy to have, his mediocrity condemning him to a life defined by classroom and mortgage, routine and monotony. Unless some miracle occurred, he had lost this flat and everything it represented as he had, so easily, so stupidly, lost Gene.

He was wide awake, more awake than he had been in months. Turning gently, he looked at the man beside him, saw his eyes were closed, saw he might be asleep, might even be dead. Alive or not, he was, at least for the moment, a stranger, next to whom Mark had no reason to lie. Gently he eased himself out from under the blankets like a snake shedding loose skin and stood up. For a moment he wondered what to do, then he walked softly through to the kitchen where he made the cup of coffee that he had earlier offered and had refused. The strangeness of his surroundings, of the need to keep silent, of the act, of the time, all combined to heighten his awareness, his sense of dislocation, so that as he took his first sip it seemed that he had never tasted coffee before, that he had never been awake so late at night, that he had never found himself with a lover sleeping, lying quietly in an adjacent room.

The partition that divided the room allowed Mark to switch on a table light so he could read without disturbing Gene. He looked through the small collection of paperbacks that were lined along the floor and chose one whose blurb suggested it would be both entertaining and interesting. Reading rapidly, he lost track of time, absorbed by the story of a Pope who believed he was the last of the line, whose duty it was to prevent the impending apocalypse and whose politicking and scheming only brought about the disasters he was trying to avoid. It seemed to Mark to be prediction rather than imagination and as he turned the pages his fear grew that civilisation would not escape, that disasters, both man-created and natural, would drown, burn and bury us all. Racing towards the end, flying over words and paragraphs, he found his attention faltering, his consciousness failing him and, much as he ached to see whether there was hope for humanity, he was forced to mark the page, put the book down and crawl back into bed.

Gene was lying on his side, breathing deeply without snoring. Mark stretched out beside him, aware that it was already morning, that daylight was slowly brightening. His eyes closed, he drifted not into sleep but into a series of frighteningly real dreams in which the forces of evil, Evil Itself, were pursuing him, or he was the Pope, surrounded by priests who mocked and disobeyed him, while Gene beckoned him from a corner and he tried and tried and tried but could not follow him. He awoke in sweat and peered at the bedside clock and saw that little time had passed; it was still early morning, the tail-end of a night that had disturbed and was still disturbing him. Not sure what to do, not sure what he was doing, he got up, searched for his clothes and pulled them on again. The faint unavoidable sounds of rustling and movement caused Gene to turn, to open his eyes and ask quietly, 'What are you doing?'

'I'm going for a walk. I can't sleep.'

'Neither can I.'

Was that a sign of hope, an indication that Gene had been as disturbed by what had happened between them as Mark himself? 'Why not?'

'I was held again.'

'Held?'

'By the feeling, the force, the. . .'

If Mark had been sceptical before, doubted Gene's vague references to the supernatural or cosmic, after the night he had just spent, the night which had not yet come to an end, hours in which it seemed he had lived more acutely than ever before, he could now only accept Gene's claim as true. There was indeed more to heaven and earth than had existed in his own blinkered philosophy. 'Are you all right?' he asked, wishing he could help, wishing he could partake.

'Yes.' Gene spoke with the effort of a man exhausted.

'Do you want to come out with me?'

'No, I think I can get to sleep now.'

But I want you to come with me. I have so little time. I have to leave this evening and I don't know when I can come back; I don't know if you want me back. 'O.K. I'll see you later.'

'Bye.' There was no warmth, no love, no affection in Gene's voice; Mark might be any casual acquaintance who was taking his leave. Mark waited a moment, hoping for more, then went out and made his way down to the street.

He walked west along the Seine, his emotions and thoughts deadened, seeing but paying little attention to the deserted city, the few cars that passed and the even rarer pedestrians. Gradually his mind, cleared by the early morning stillness, the freshness of the air, focused on himself and Gene as if he understood them both for the first time. He had lost Gene, he knew; his only hope now lay in persuading him that he could change, that he was indeed changing, that the worrying and insecure Mark that Gene had seen was the last gasp of a dying man, that the Mark who returned from this walk would be another person, someone strong, self-confident, talented, someone Gene could respect, would want to be with.

He looked up to see he had reached the Eiffel Tower and was wondering how much further he would have to go to reach the Bois de Boulogne when it occurred to him that there was no reason to go on, that he had to return as quickly as possible, to show Gene that everything was different, was as if they had just met, as if the process of getting to know each other, of falling in love, was about to begin. He turned to walk back the way he had come, his pace now firm, almost hurried as he noticed absently that the day was already warmer, that there were more

130

cars on the streets and pedestrians out to stroll. He felt a sudden affection for them, for this city, an outpouring of his confidence, his determination that all would be well. Striding on, he looked forward to seeing Gene with greater eagerness than ever before.

His new-found confidence had not won Gene back but it had, in the months that followed, led to a Mark that was different in substance if not in type, like a nervous kitten grown into a resolute if cautious cat. Moreover it had, sometimes without his being aware of it, helped him to get over Gene, to draw Carl and to tolerate the weeks and months of Carl's rejection. It was that confidence which had made him in the end the stronger, more reliable partner in their relationship, the same confidence which he had never succeeded in instilling in Carl himself.

Yet the word was wrong in connection with Carl; it was not confidence he lacked but ambition, the belief that he either could or should spend his days other than preparing meals and washing dishes in Mark's flat and pulling pints and washing glasses in the bar. 'What's wrong with that?' he asked when Mark, tired of dropping hints that were never taken up, of casually pointing the conversation in directions that Carl would never follow, criticised him for allowing himself to be used, for aiming for no more than he already had. 'Don't you want me to cook for you?' he went on, as if surprised by the thought.

'I want you to cook if you're willing to do it, but I'd be happier if you were doing something else.'

'Like what?'

'Like a course.'

'You said that before. I'm not interested. I've done enough courses.'

And passed them; Carl had his weaknesses, but lack of intelligence was not one of them. 'You told me,' said Mark. 'Maybe they were wrong for you. But if you want to manage your own bar. . .'

'Who said I wanted to?'

'You did.'

'I said I could. I didn't say I wanted to.'

131

'Why not?'

'What's the point?'

'More money. Be your own boss. . .' Mark's voice trailed off as he realised he himself did not know why Carl should follow that path, only that it seemed the right thing to do.

'It would just mean harder work and more responsibility. I don't want it.'

'So you just want to be a bartender for the rest of your life.'

'I don't know! What does it matter?' Carl responded, irritation entering his voice.

I don't want to spend the rest of my life with a barman, with a houseboy, with someone who has no greater ambition than to be my slave. But those were comments that Mark feared to whisper to himself, far less state openly to Carl. 'I don't like to see you wasting yourself, wasting your time.'

'I'm not. I'm happy. I'm happy with you; I'm happy doing what I'm doing. Now will you leave it, please? I don't go on at you, tell you you should be a headmaster or something like that.'

'Perhaps you should. Perhaps you should nag me about my songs.'

'Why should I?'

'Then maybe I'd get down to writing more, getting them recorded, getting them sold.'

'But if that's what you really wanted, you'd do it all without me.' Sometimes Carl came uncomfortably close to the truth.

'Maybe I need you to push me.'

'How?'

'Ask me every night you come home how many songs I've written, how many producers or agents I've seen.'

'O.K., I'll nag you three times a day. "Mark, have you been signed by EMI? Mark, when are you appearing on Top of the Pops? Mark, how much money have you made today?" Will that do?' Carl grinned, looking for approval. Yet even as he was speaking Mark knew that if Carl were to make the effort to do as he was asked it would only be by rote and with no understanding of what his lover was trying to do, with the result that Mark would be shamed not into writing, into trying to sell his songs, but into making excuses, into getting annoyed. What would inspire Mark would not be Carl off-handedly pushing him from behind but Carl rushing on ahead, achieving his own goals and turning round to say, whether explicitly or not, 'This is mine; now show me what's yours.' Instead, life with Carl stretched before him as dull and predictable as his school timetable. Surely now, with all the early rows, misunderstandings and pain behind them, they should be moving on. The next step should be Mark giving up teaching, forcing himself to become a full-time performer and writer, while Carl overcame his reluctance and found a pub or nightclub to manage. Then later, after two or three years, they would buy one of those bars in Greece or Spain that Carl had mentioned, which made their owners not only enough in six months of the holiday season to do nothing for the rest of the year but also to invest a sizeable amount to allow them to retire early. Mark would spend his days by the swimming-pool of their private villa composing and his nights entertaining in the small but crowded bar where Carl and one or two handsome young assistants were kept busy until dawn. He had once tried to pin down the idea, to get Carl to commit himself to a future time and place, but the more enthusiastic he had become, the less interest Carl had shown, until Mark reluctantly had to accept that not only was the bar with its background of beach and sun a dream for Carl but, like any dream, it was one that he neither expected nor particularly wanted to become a reality.

Mark's frustration grew slowly, unnoticed, over weeks. He found the few hours of free time that he shared with Carl given up again and again in return for the promise, sincerely made but almost never fulfilled, of Carl's yielding at a later date to whatever he, Mark, wanted to do. Thus if they went out it was to a restaurant, not a cinema; if they played music it was the latest hit rather than classical or folk; if they watched television it was soap opera not a documentary. If Carl's choices had been the expression of someone who was incapable of appreciating the deeper or more serious aspects of life and art, Mark would have been disappointed but would have accepted the situation, perhaps wondering occasionally how he had become involved with someone with whom he could never have anything in common. Then he would have expected and demanded a clearer distinction between his own life and life with his lover, insisting that there were times when he had to be alone, when he had to be free to do what he wanted. But Carl was by no means unintelligent, indeed he demonstrated at times a clearer understanding of people and situations than Mark, and had been, it appeared, a brighter than average student. In Mark's eyes there was no reason why he could not train himself to enjoy what Mark enjoyed; all that held him back was laziness, the lack of ambition that Mark always stumbled over, the desire to be no more than a popular and efficient barman, Mark's housekeeper and his lover.

Carl had never changed, never understood Mark's unhappiness and dissatisfaction. He must have seen the signs and decided to ignore them, hoping that Mark's state of mind was, like his own confusion of a year before, a storm that could be ridden out and survived. The storm, however, had been too great and Carl had proved too rigid, too stubborn while Mark was too weak, too flexible for them to be able to hold on to each other, for them not to be tossed apart. When the end had come he only knew that he, Mark, had survived; as for Carl, he would never know.

He sat down again at the piano and played the melody that he had developed so far, elaborating here and there with bass chords, going back when words and music did not quite match, experimenting with the rhythm. It was not difficult – unlike other songs where the ideas obstinately refused to be moulded into lyrics or notes that sounded dull, lifeless, unrelated to what he wanted to say – and soon he picked up his pen and started to jot down the music, letting it emerge from under his hand as if a film had been reversed and the stains he was wiping away had reappeared. Every so often he stopped, played and sang what had been written, then worked on until after an hour the piano's part was complete, and scribbled above or below were reminders for the harmony, strings and percussion that would come when and if they could be afforded. Finally he played the whole song through once more, starting softly, building up to a crescendo – 'and the branches reach down like the arms of her mother, wrap themselves round like the arms of her lover' – dying to the coda of the man who searches for her 'and stands among the trees seeing her shadow in the leaves,' and he sat back, content.

He wanted Robert to be here, now, so he could grab hold of him, kiss him, say look, listen, it's good, it's good. He would play it once more with Robert standing over him, his hands resting on Mark's shoulders, a thumb or finger gently stroking the back of his neck or behind his ear and listen to Mark singing it again, altering it slightly, prolonging one note, shortening another, adding an echo, a trill, giving the whole yet more depth, more emotion and Robert would recognise how good it was, recognise he had a lover who was as talented as he was himself. But Robert wasn't here, was having lunch or was already at the hall or theatre talking about yesterday's performance or preparing for the next. Again Mark reluctantly wondered if he were at the centre of Robert's thoughts, if every moment that Robert was neither on stage nor in class Mark filled his mind, whether as a figure of reassuring warmth or a symbol of awe and remoteness. He suspected, however, as he always did, that even if Robert's attention was free to wander, if he were sitting alone in some café or off stage, it would not be towards London that his thoughts would look but into whatever book he had to hand, absorbed more by the emotions he found there than by those he felt. Then someone would call his name and he would look up as if woken from sleep, reminded that it was time to go over to the theatre or, if he were already there, to get on stage, and he would push himself up from whichever corner he had been squatting in, stretch like a cat, a lion or a tiger, and re-enter the world of dance, the world he was part of, the world that before Mark, before anything, he loved.

He would have forgotten the incident of the tape, as Mark realised he himself had forgotten it. The emotions of self-recrimination and fear that had haunted him all Saturday had died in last night's sleep, the whole episode from the moment he had reached into Robert's bag for the small plastic case to the cold discussion which had ended Friday night, now seemed part of a past that affected him little more than abstract history. He still felt the same doubt towards Robert, wondered how much he cared, wondered if he would call that night, wondered how each would behave when they next met; but that doubt was greater, was somehow rooted in more than a simple cassette. The tape, Mark realised, was irrelevant, no more than a symbol of their different concerns and needs; at some point, whether the catalyst was the cassette or Robert's once again forgetting to call or insisting on going home, there was certain to be conflict, manifestation of the tension that could not be avoided when Robert's preference, perhaps his need, for isolation met Mark's hunger to be with him, his reluctance to be alone.

In that respect Robert was like Gene, from which the logical conclusion came that he and Mark would not stay together either. The comparison, while chilling Mark, did not frighten him; he had matured in the past two years and, while he could still argue with his lover, hurt and be hurt by him, he was no longer capable of alienating himself, of displaying such weakness, such insecurity that had once caused him almost deliberately to push Gene away. If then he had realised his mistake too late, he had at least learned never to be so foolish, so selfishly self-destructive again.

He had arrived back that morning at about seven o'clock, opened the flat door as quietly as he could and padded through to the bedroom where Gene was not sitting up, waiting, wondering, worrying where Mark had gone, but was indeed sleeping, the sound of light snoring rising and falling with the blankets that covered him. The old Mark wanted to kneel on the bed, to shake Gene into consciousness, to plead with him, to beg him to say that everything was all right, that he could crawl in beside him, that they could make love or fall asleep again together, but the new Mark realised all that was wrong: all he could do was wait for Gene to wake, make another coffee and sit by the window, finish the book he had started in the middle of the night, and stare down at the street, which had never lost its unfamiliarity, which was still to him welcome and strange.

He picked up the paperback and tried to follow the story but the connection between his ability to read and his ability to understand had broken and the words made no more sense than if they had been cut up and replaced at random on the page. Putting it aside, he found himself abstractly watching Gene, a figure buried under the covers like an ancient temple hidden by the centuries under an earthen mound. His mind was blank; the effort of staying awake had drained him of energy; his thoughts had come to a halt as quietly as a car running out of petrol, a machine dying in a power cut. He no longer knew what he felt for Gene, could remember their first meeting but not the warmth that had accompanied it, as he remembered the night that had just passed but none of the emotions that had thrilled and frightened him. All he knew was that he had to be here, had to watch and wait until Gene awoke, when his, Mark's, mind would laboriously creak and clank into action, take in sentences and words, gestures and tone, process them and slowly respond with his own speech and emotions.

When Gene turned, however, opened his eyes and saw Mark watching him, all he did was mutter 'Come to bed'. As if he had been unable to move before that invitation, Mark pulled off his clothes and crawled in beside him, aware of the cold stiffness of his own body against Gene's supple warmth. He wanted, expected to hold and be held, kiss and be kissed, but he did not even put an arm over Gene before falling asleep, into a deep, dark and dreamless state from which he emerged hours later. Finding himself alone, he turned and saw, one after the other, Gene at his easel and the bedside clock standing at noon. Shocked fully awake by the realisation that in a few hours he would have gone, he was about to speak, but heard Gene asking how he had slept.

'Fine.' With the word came memory of the previous night, as complete, three-dimensional and startling as a perfect hologram, the structure of each event coloured by a different emotion, Gene's or his own. Equally strong was his new mood, his determination to keep Gene, to proceed with the care and fearlessness of a tightrope-walker across an abyss of death and failure.

'There's coffee,' Gene said.

But you're not going to bring it to me. Well, I can't expect everything. 'Thanks. Where?'

'In the kitchen.' Gene turned back to his work. 'Do you mind keeping quiet for a little? I have to finish this off.'

'How long?'

'An hour.'

So long? I have to leave at nine; Mark stifled the once automatic response. 'Sure.'

'Then we can go out for lunch.'

'If you want I can cook something here.'

Gene shook his head, the conversation, the audience, over.

Coffee and a slice of bread in hand Mark sat in the opposite corner, out of the light, out of Gene's vision, and picked up the book he had not yet finished. Now that he was properly awake, refreshed, its power to hold him, to reach into the deepest part of his psyche and suggest this is all prophecy, it's all true, our lives are meaningless, the world will end this way, had faded and he saw it as no more than a competently written story, one consciously crafted but with little soul. When he had come to the end, he put it aside with a shrug, more disappointed than satisfied and looked over at Gene.

'That's that,' Gene said eventually, taking a cloth and wiping his brush.

'Is it finished?' Mark asked, walking over and looking closely at the work for the first time. Dark eyes peered out at him from a flat, oval, thinly featured face. He had

138

no idea whether what he was seeing was a work of art or amateurishness.

Gene nodded.

'What are you going to do with it?'

'Try and sell it.'

'Who to?'

'I don't know.' Although the intonation and pitch were unchanged, Gene's voice was hollow, lacked the warmth of yesterday, of Mark's previous visits; was the voice of one being polite to a perfect stranger. He stood up, went through to the kitchen and washed his hands while Mark stayed with his eyes on the woman.

'Where do you want to go for lunch?' Gene asked, coming back into the room.

'You choose.'

'You're on holiday here.'

Is that all? Just a holiday? Mark felt that the solid ground he was standing on was crumbling into a swift and flooding river into which he might at any moment fall. 'What about somewhere expensive? I'll pay,' he offered. To make up for last night, to try to win you back.

'I don't know anywhere expensive. Anyway, what's the point?'

'Well, let's just go for a walk and see what we come across.'

The sun was shining but a light breeze kept the day cool. They wandered towards Montmartre, idly comparing Paris and London like guests at a party who do not know each other but are willing to pass the time together until their own friends come. There was, almost palpable, a barrier between them, thin and transparent, which allowed them to see and talk to each other but not to hold and touch. Mark tried to overcome it but his words slipped out of control like a toehold on ice, leaving him floundering, rattling on about the Northern Line and rush-hour crowds when he wanted to be saying hey, let's not talk about that, let's talk about you and me, the fact that I'm different, let's eat quickly and go back to the flat and make love.

Eventually they found a moderately busy, moderately priced restaurant in a narrow street and were given a table

139

by the window where they could look out at the small groups of tourists who occasionally passed. There was an American couple by the door and an English family with complaining children in a corner, but the other diners appeared to be French, and Mark sat with Gene as if in welcome isolation.

'I'm tired,' he said when they had ordered and were waiting for the first course. 'Are you?' Perhaps now he could gently, carefully, bring their thoughts back to themselves.

'A little.'

'What happened last night?'

'What do you mean?'

'You said you were "held"?'

'It's nothing.'

'But I'm interested to know.'

Gene shook his head and Mark fought down the urge to complain, to demand to be told. If something extraordinary could happen to Gene, whether it was wonderful or terrible, real or a figment of his imagination, Mark wanted to know about it, wanted it to be shared, to undergo it himself. He could, however, say nothing, could only force himself to change the subject. 'I read that book.'

'The one about the Pope?'

'Yes.'

'I thought it was good.'

'So did I. At one point I thought it was all real.'

'Maybe it is,' said Gene, but his comment was automatic, a dampener not an invitation to further discussion.

'What are you going to paint next?' Mark asked, aware of the effort it took to be bright, friendly, insouciant.

'I'm not sure.'

'Me?'

Gene smiled weakly, but said nothing.

'Maybe I'll put you in my next song. Make you a romantic figure who struggles on his own for years. Or who achieves fame and fortune and throws it all away.' His words sounded flat, almost an insult.

'I don't think I'll be either.' Gene looked up as the waiter brought their wine.

For the rest of the meal Mark teetered between the tiredness that made him want to do no more than finish the meal, go back to the flat and sleep and the tension that kept him alert, on the look-out for the first sign that Gene was relenting, that the crisis was past, that he recognised he was in the presence of a new, improved Mark. Their conversation, however, continued to be as brittle as when it began, and by the time the coffee came he had come no closer to Gene, had been compelled to keep a distance as if he were in a museum staring at a beautiful artefact that was for ever out of touch. When they left and Mark voiced his assumption that they were going back to the flat, Gene said sure, if Mark was tired he should go lie down, but he himself wanted to stay out, to stroll around Montmartre and later take the metro to Père Lachaise. Of course Mark would not leave Gene, preferred to accompany him, even silently, through back-streets and along cemetery paths where, as the afternoon wore on, his awareness of his surroundings, the warm sun, the stillness despite the breeze, his tall companion, was tempered by regret, by memory of last night; and a new emotion was engendered, a bitter-sweetness that allowed him to accept that he had lost Gene while making these few last hours together as pleasant, as intense, as the first day they had met.

They arrived back at the flat after six, allowing time for Gene to prepare a light meal while Mark packed the few things that he seemed only to have unpacked a few hours before. After eating in silence, washing and putting the few dishes away, Mark looked at the clock, saw it was early, but knew that Gene was waiting for him to go. 'I'll leave,' he said. 'You don't have to come to the station, you know.'

'I'll come.'

Mark put on his jacket, bent down to pick up his bag, glanced round to check that he had left nothing. Gene watched him, expressionless.

'Gene . . . I'm sorry about last night. I didn't mean to annoy you.'

141

'It's O.K. We all need to let it out sometimes.' For the first time that day there was warmth in Gene's words.

'Yes, but it's unfair to take it out on someone else.'

Gene shrugged.

'Thank you,' Mark said, putting his arms round Gene, not sure what he was thanking him for, not sure how he would react to this embrace.

Gene hugged him briefly, as an uncle, a brother. 'Let's go.'

It was easier at the station than he had expected. They were early, but Gene was willing to sit and have coffee, to nod or comment as Mark, somehow relaxed, relieved, talked about school and told anecdotes of pupils he had already mentioned to Gene. When he casually referred to the next time he would be in Paris, as if there were no question that in two or three weeks he would be back and everything would continue as before, Gene said nothing, did not discourage him, and he allowed his spirits to leap, to believe that the crisis was past, that all each of them needed was time to recover and they could and would continue as lovers, closer and happier than before.

It had been as easy to deceive himself then as it had been with Carl, easy to see and hear only what he wanted to hear, to draw only the optimistic conclusions, to ignore or belittle the real problems which, under his nose, were pulling them apart. With Gene he had brought out into the open thoughts and emotions that should have been left unspoken, difficulties that were for Mark alone to resolve. With Carl he had kept silent, given his lover little idea of what was going on in his mind, of the thoughts and emotions which did not concern him alone but affected them both. Thus while Carl was at work Mark had at last started to go out on his own, seeing plays or films or visiting friends as Carl had always said he should, but also spending time in gay bars, watching the other customers but seldom talking to them, wondering why they were here, whether they were alone or, like him, had lovers at home. Automatically he looked out for the occasional young man who attracted him, looked him

142

over, sometimes allowed a flicker of interest to pass between their eyes, but he never approached the stranger, always surrendered to the excuse that the other was with someone or time was passing and he had to get home rather than acknowledge that what held him back, what was the true reason for his hesitancy, was the promise he had once made to Carl.

Mark's greatest emotion towards the end of their relationship was disappointment, a residue of the frustration that he used to feel. The difference may have been that earlier he had thought the situation could change, that he and Carl could consciously change it, whereas now he realised that nothing would change, that the rut they had fallen into, not only of work and time but of emotion and dependency, was too deep, too difficult to climb out of. There were compensations, Mark knew, but what had satisfied him in the past meant little now, was a sop to keep a starving man alive, not food that gave a healthy man strength. If he found himself looking at other men, a reflex that had lain dormant in most of the first year of living with Carl, it was indeed with the wish to have sex, but that desire only masked a deeper, less clearly formulated need to communicate on levels that were barred between himself and Carl. Or was he merely rationalising, dressing up the starkness of his sexual drive in more acceptable clothes? If what Mark really wanted from another man was a good, sweaty no-holds-barred night at the National Theatre followed by an hour's nit-picking at the bar, Carl would not complain, would encourage him to go out, would even be pleased that someone could give him what he himself could not. If Mark needed a guitarist or a drummer, someone to accompany him or prod him into writing, into writing more, writing better, again Carl would not object, would indeed be proud that his lover was a song-writer heading towards fame. Carl did not want Mark's intellect nor all his time; he asked for nothing more than sexual and emotional fidelity as the price of his love and that, Mark realised, might be more than he could give.

In those winter months Mark might be greedy and

want his lover to embody every one of his ideals, to be the intellectual and the whore, the humorist and the housekeeper, the self-contained adult and the affectionate teenager, but he did not yet seriously consider giving up a relationship that only partly satisfied him. After all he was still in love, still enjoyed making the gestures of affection, the spontaneous kiss or unexpected gift, even if they had become rarer, actions he had to remind himself of rather than automatic reflexes. And Carl still freely and unreservedly loved him, broke into a broad smile each time they met, hugged him, was happy at any time and in any place just to be with him, made love with the same tenderness and eagerness as they had on their first night. Mark could no more think of throwing it all away than he could imagine cutting off an arm or an ear on which some unattractive but harmless mole had begun to grow. Carl was part of his life and if that life was losing its thrill he should not, he could not, complain.

Yet what his mind could rationalise his emotions would not accept. He found himself sometimes impatient or bored, at other times lonely even when not alone, and although he tried to disguise those feelings it finally became obvious to Carl that something was wrong. Rather than speak, however, ask Mark what the problem might be, his concern showed itself in the more care he took, greater solicitude, and the silent way his presence hovered around Mark like a lively dog temporarily subdued by his master's mood. More than once he came home from the pub slightly drunk, a state Mark could accept when it was manifest in humour and gossip, but an extra drink or an extra hour would turn the mood sour and Carl would complain that Mark had not come to visit him, had preferred to go to some film, to pick someone up. Mark could laugh off the last accusation the first time it was made, but if it was repeated he could not prevent himself from becoming angry, from responding so what if he did, the opening words of an unwelcome but familiar argument. Then, regretting his reaction, regretting the pain it caused, he would talk into the night trying to convince Carl, trying to convince himself, that he would

144

never do such a thing, that everything between them was all right, that his restlessness was just a phase he was going through, one that would soon pass. Finally, in the early hours of the morning they would make love to seal the contract that Mark had carefully restated and fall asleep exhausted, only recovering from the ordeal and returning to their habitual interaction the following day.

What most surprised Mark towards the end was the way in which sex between them changed. As his interest in Carl waned, the handsome face and invitingly thick hair no longer compensating for a body that was uncared for and rough to the touch, his compassion for Carl grew and he found himself unable to refuse to make love, to push Carl away, to insist on either falling asleep or the sop of quick masturbation. Their unspoken rule of taking turns in penetration was set aside and Mark allowed himself to be almost every time the partner who lay back, who opened himself up, who sometimes offered more than he received. It was, he realised later, an act of penance, an apology, seeking forgiveness for the adultery he sought but had not the courage to commit. And whether Carl was aware of this, was consciously or not extracting his due, Mark found that the act no longer gave him much pleasure; it lasted much longer than he either expected or desired and became an ordeal, something to tolerate, to grit his teeth at, like a lesson with a difficult class in which he would achieve little more than a headache. Only once, the weekend before he had met Robert, when, both relaxed, at ease with each other, they had made love in the afternoon, had the overwhelming sensation reciprocated that was both physical and emotional, both gross sensuality and deep love; he had looked up at the face bending over him like a concerned angel and felt the warmth and weight within him that he never wanted to lose and silently begged that it could always be like this, that they would never leave each other.

At its best, sex with Carl had been good but seldom more than that, hampered at first by Carl's lack of imagination, his seeing little beyond the need to be gentle and take care, and later by Mark's diminishing interest, his motive more guilt than affection. It had nevertheless been an improvement on the few hours spent with Gene after the love-making of his first visit had been replaced by the energetic but ultimately – for Mark – unfulfilling sex in which they were as much undeclared aggressors as partners. Only looking back did it occur to him that Gene's avoidance of intercourse, his claim that it was uncomfortable, was an indication that he was already losing interest in Mark, saw him as no more than a casual partner. Or was that thought both unfounded and unfair? The break between them had come much later; Gene was just one of these people whose sexual needs differed from his own. Perhaps if they had stayed together Mark might have weaned him off his insistence on sparring like adolescent boys uncertain, half-afraid, of their burgeoning sexual drives and only able to express it in contest, in attack and submission. Probably not, probably even if they had lived in the same city their relationship would have broken up as quickly as it did, for Gene's self-containment, his intolerance of any weakness had nothing to do with the infrequency with which they saw each other. Yet Gene's reluctance to perform, to enjoy, the complete sexual act was in Mark's eyes itself a weakness, an inability to give himself completely, an immaturity, a refusal to accept and offer total responsibility for himself and his actions.

Or was that another gum-tree he was barking up as he had barked up so many before? Robert and he made love often and seldom with more than mouths and hands. Partly because Robert was often tired, even after a night's rest, and the act of copulation seemed too energetic and partly because somehow it seemed unnecessary; after an hour of kissing, of stroking, of exploring, of discovering the sensitivity of chest, of arms, of thighs, of neck, playing with that sensitivity, building it up into a delicate crescendo in which Robert would moan and tremble beneath him, knowing that Robert was experiencing a sensation as intense as any orgasm yet free of any coarse manipulation of his erection, was to Mark both the greatest gift he could offer and the greatest reward he could receive. It was true love-making for it went beyond the purely animal goal of orgasm, made orgasm irrelevant – welcome if it occurred, but nonetheless irrelevant.

But to get to that stage one had to go through the preceding stages of routine orgasm and penetration, which were thresholds, keys, passwords that led from the first curious glances to falling in, being in, love. And now, should he ever part from Robert, these stages were beset by far greater obstacles than, when young and uncertain, he had made love. He was not sure now when he had first heard of AIDS, but there had been a period when AIDS threatened to reduce the warmth and sharing he sought in intercourse to the solitary action that was its substitute; at times it seemed that he and whoever he had met were held apart by fear, standing at opposite ends of the bedroom where, desperate yet unable to hold each other, to kiss or make love, they masturbated furiously like disturbed mental patients, like frustrated and lonely adolescents. He accepted condoms reluctantly, otherwise refusing to let the disease dominate his life as it seemed to dominate the lives of so many others. On learning that David had fallen ill, he had sympathised but in his heart could see it as no more significant than any other tragedy, a paralysing car accident, a rare leukaemia that was the result more of chance than one's own actions. What he resented most of all was the suggestion that alternative forms of sex – doing A, avoiding B and discouraging C – were as valid as those that had gone before. For others perhaps, but for him the effect of all that well-meaning advice was to reduce sex to no more than friction, to secretive childhood memories of masturbation, to the level of rutting dogs excited by whatever objects rubbed against their skin. The greatest aspect of love was the tearing away of all restrictions between lovers, of intimacy with every aspect of each other's personalities and bodies. Whether one died from it was almost irrelevant – you did not refrain from walking along the street because some car might crash into you, a building fall, a terrorist bomb explode. So he and Carl had talked of taking the test, hoping to find themselves both negative or both positive so they could make love with truly nothing between them, but had broken up before

147

the decision was taken. Whether Robert and he would ever reach such intimacy Mark did not know, but at the back of his mind it was the goal, the pinnacle of love that he wanted to reach.

An ache in his stomach interrupted his thoughts, made him realise that it was already mid-afternoon and he was hungry again. He stood up and went through to the kitchen, where, as ever lacking the imagination to cook, he fried an egg and bacon, heated beans and made toast. He ate in the living-room watching an old film where Ellery Queen, with the broad cheeks and wide mouth considered handsome in the thirties, nonchalantly solved a series of murders in a Californian house. When it was over, and the criminal, an insane old man in swimming costume and training shoes, apprehended and the heroine kissed, he switched off and went over to look at his song for the last time that day, to see if it was as good as he told himself it was.

He sat at the piano, propped the sheets of scribbled paper on the stand, made himself comfortable and turned to an imaginary audience, seeing himself, for lack of any other model, as a more down-to-earth and more serious Noel Coward. 'I'd like to play you now,' he began hoarsely and cleared his throat, 'I'd like to play you now my latest song, "Hyde Park". I hope you enjoy it.' No, he thought as he played the opening chords, that was too stiff, he'd have to learn to relax, put a bit of warmth in his voice. 'One warm afternoon in a half-empty park. . .' As he played, his mind darted a few bars ahead, suggesting different notes, changed emphases, which he incorporated without hearing clearly how well they sounded. When he came to the end, he started again, this time playing exactly what he had written, and tried to project himself across the room, to be not the performer but the audience. Yes, it sounded good, and no, there would never be a definitive version, because it would change according to the mood he was in; the wistfulness he was giving it today could easily yield at other times to sentiment or bitterness. But it was most certainly a song he could add to his repertoire, a song that should be on The Tape, one that was much better than the simple love ballads he had written years ago. Perhaps he could make another tape, just of that song, to hawk round the studios. And perhaps now he had enough material to put on his own show; he no longer had the excuse that he was held back from performing by his refusal to perform others' songs.

As for The Tape, the copy he had taken back from Robert still lay on the chair in the bedroom where he had dropped it on Tuesday untouched as if it were white hot or alive with electricity. Remembering it, his guilt returned, guilt that he had given in to a moment of weak pride, that he had hurt Robert; the anger, however, he still considered justified, the vague but deep-rooted belief that he had been let down, somehow betrayed. That anger was quieter now, a torrent dwindled to a slow-moving stream, but on Tuesday its violence had shaken him for most of the day.

He had called Robert in the morning before going to school to see if he was free that night. He wasn't; he had made other plans.

'What?'

'I'm going out with some friends.'

Can't I come? The words almost slipped out. 'Anyone I know?'

'No. They're from New York; they're only here for a few days.'

'How come you know them?'

'They saw me dance a couple of years ago. We've kept in touch.'

'As long as they don't actually touch.' Mark regretted the words, that the humour was weaker than the implied jealousy.

'They're a married couple.'

'But they know you're gay.'

'No,' Robert said. 'Why should they?'

'Why shouldn't they?'

'It's nothing to do with them.'

'Where are you going?'

'For a meal probably. Maybe the cinema.'

'So I can't see you tonight.' Mark was becoming aware

that the effort to maintain a light tone masked a growing resentment.

'No.'

'When will we next meet?' We, together; not I, selfish.

'Not till Friday. I've got classes and rehearsals every day.'

'That'll be almost a week and then you're going away.' Mark tried to keep the complaint, the whine, out of his voice.

'I know. I can't help it.'

'Don't you have any free time today?'

'I finish at four. Then I've got to go home and change.'

'What about a coffee beforehand?'

'O.K.' Robert's voice was neutral, the aural equivalent of a shrug.

'McDonalds? Baker Street? Quarter past four?'

'O.K. I really have to go now.'

'See you then. Break a leg.'

'I probably will.'

It was only when Mark had put the receiver down that the nervousness provoked by the need to appear adult, mature, non-possessive, all the positive qualities that he sometimes felt and always wished to present, gave way to an anger that spilled out in all the questions that he had not asked and had not thought to ask. Why didn't you invite me, why can't I come, are you ashamed of me, am I someone you have to hide from your better friends, do I only get to meet the other dancers – the ones that aren't good enough to threaten you, don't I have a right to be with you? He stared at the phone for a moment, wondering whether to pick it up again, to stab out Robert's number, to demand that as his lover he go out with him that night, with his friends or alone, and was only held back by a quiet voice telling him no, that such an action would only have the opposite effect, would surprise Robert, jolt him, as Gene had been jolted, into seeing a new Mark, one who was weak and prey to jealousy and anger.

But he was angry, dammit! His fist swung down in a melodramatic gesture that pounded the table and bounced

150

the telephone towards the edge. What did Robert's protestation of love mean if every time they could be, should be together he made an excuse to go home, to be somewhere else, to claim he was tired, he was busy, couldn't be free? It was all very well Mark being the ideal lover, offering everything, insisting on nothing, being patient and understanding and undemanding if Robert offered nothing in return, if he graciously doled out the gift of his presence in meagre rations like the Queen bestowing useless coins on Maundy Thursday, offering to spend the night here or go out to the cinema there but never going further, never saying, hey lover, I want to move in with you, kick out that dreary old lodger, I want his room, or yes, I'll come home with you tonight and tomorrow night, I'll tell my mother something, it doesn't matter what, and we'll make love and I'll get up early and bring you tea in the morning and then we'll leave together, you for school and me for class and we'll meet again at night and, and. . .

Mark's thoughts were interrupted by the realisation that it was late, that he would have to hurry, and his ire dwindled like a fountain losing pressure as he made a quick toilet, checked the contents of his briefcase, left the flat and strode down the stairs and out into the street. It was not until the middle of the morning, when he was sitting in the staff-room during a free period correcting a series of dull essays, that his attention wandered and the morning's phone call and the emotions it aroused flooded back into his mind. His anger was calmer now but no less strong; the wild exclamations and rhetorical questions that had ricocheted around his mind giving way to seemingly implacable reasons. If he loves me he should not behave like that, therefore I have every right to be angry, therefore I have every right to tell him he is wrong. He has upset me, therefore I have every right to upset him, therefore I have to punish him in some way. As he argued himself into knots the heat of his rage began to grip him again like a fever, so that it seemed that his whole body had been taken over until it vibrated, seethed with outrage. At its centre, the one calming influence, was the belief, the certainty that when Robert saw and understood what he had done, how much he had hurt Mark, he would be so unhappy, so regretful – Mark could already hear the words of apology, see the tears stream down Robert's face – that Mark's anger, his righteous anger, would be drowned in the forgiveness that would well up and spill out and overwhelm them both.

Returning to the classroom dispelled Mark's immediate emotions as efficiently as an aspirin relieving a headache without soothing away the underlying tensions. By the time he left school, however, the approaching meeting with Robert was a cold wind of reality that blew down like a house of cards the faith he had in himself and in the logic of the conversation he had rehearsed. Even if he was right – even though he was right – to feel that Robert had behaved badly, selfishly, to attack and accuse him like an authoritarian parent, a weary headmaster, a lecturing judge, would only alienate, destroy the image of himself that Mark so wanted to maintain, the image of a wise, forgiving and understanding lover.

Robert was already there, idly stirring a coffee, staring at the back of a girl a few feet away as if he could see projected onto her jacket new steps, new choreography, the outlines of his next role. When Mark approached, he looked up with a smile of welcome which transformed Mark's mood from difficult duty to unstrained pleasure, reminding him, although he did not need to be reminded, that whatever his thoughts, his emotions might be they were irrelevant; all he wanted from life was to be with Robert, to be in his presence, talking, making love, even sitting for ever silent.

'A good day?' he asked, sitting with coffee before him.

'Mm,' Robert nodded. 'Not bad. How about you?'

'Routine. Are you tired?'

'No more than usual.'

'So tell me about these people you're meeting tonight.' The words came out before he could stop them, before he could search for something innocuous to say.

'The Merrivales? They're just some people I met a couple

of years ago. They come to London about once or twice a year.'

'They saw you dance.' He wanted to sound casual, but heard himself as an interrogator, an inquisitor.

'She's a friend of one of my teachers. The class was putting on a performance and I was introduced to them afterwards. Then we all had dinner.'

'Are they dancers?'

'She used to be until she broke her foot. Something happened; it didn't set properly.'

'Where are you going tonight?' He had to stop asking these questions, yet he could not. The need to know everything, to floodlight the next few hours, to search out and examine every possibility, to assure himself that there was nothing hidden, no secret Robert did not wish to reveal, over-rode Mark's fear that all he was doing was revealing his own weakness and insecurity.

'I don't know. I'm meeting them at their hotel at eight. Then we'll probably go for a meal somewhere.'

'Where are they staying?'

'The Hilton.'

So these friends had money and connections and, knowing Robert, most probably wit and discrimination. What hurt, offended, upset Mark was not that they were a threat, competing for Robert's affections, but that Robert for some reason did not see him as worthy to meet them, considered his lover as someone who had to be kept in the background, out of sight and, no doubt, out of conversation. Yet if they were indeed lovers, Mark had a right to be with Robert, to share his life, his friendships; had at least the right to be inquired after, to be someone that Robert showed interest in. Go on, he thought, trying to project into Robert's mind; ask me what I'm doing tonight, how I'm going to spend my time, or ask me to come out with you, prove to me how important our relationship is.

But Robert said nothing, sat twirling the plastic stirrer with his usual half-smile.

'I've got a lot of correction to do,' Mark said in a last attempt to break through to Robert, to let him see how important this issue was, 'but I was thinking of ignoring it and going to the cinema tonight.'

'What film?'

'I'm not sure. Probably *Wild Strawberries*; I've never seen it.'

'You'll love it. I cried.'

Mark shrugged, suddenly angry at his failure, at Robert's obtuseness. 'Have you listened to my tape?'

Robert shook his head. 'I haven't had time.'

'Well, listen to it soon.' Or I'll think you don't care. I'm not even sure if you deserve to listen to it now. 'Are you looking forward to the weekend?'

'It's just a try-out.'

'Why isn't it a full tour?'

'Because none of us can get the time away. And Margaret knows the director there, offered him this new work. There are other possibilities in a month or so.'

The conversation tailed off. For a moment their attention was taken by watching those around them, schoolchildren playing and shoving each other, office girls gossiping, an Arab family sitting silently, the husband staring into space, the wife feeding the small girl on her lap. 'I'll be back in a minute,' Robert said, standing up and making for the toilet.

That had been the moment in which it had occurred to Mark that what he must do was take back the tape, that the discovery of its loss would convey to Robert more than any words of Mark's how he felt, how deeply he had been wounded. Now, less than a week later, his perspective had changed; he could see how stupid he had been, how much more he had expected of Robert than Robert was able to give. Yes, Mark resented the moments when he felt cut out of Robert's life, the time that was sacrificed not to Mark but to class, to rehearsal, to going home, but there had never been any suggestion that Robert was losing interest in him, that there was someone else in his life, a rival for his affections, a handsome, talented or witty suitor for whom Robert would make time in an already crowded schedule, for whom he would carve out infatuation from an already committed emotion.

154

In expecting Robert to attend to his every need Mark had expected too much, not merely of a nineteen-year-old, no matter how precocious he might be, but of any lover. Instead of complaining, of feeling unloved, it would be wiser to remember that when he had had such devotion, when Carl had been with him, had wanted to be with him every minute of every day, he had found it too much, too stifling, like an overheated room from which one longs to escape, at least temporarily, to the cool, even the cold, breeze outside.

But with Carl, once the door had been opened it could not be shut; the warmth fled and to turn, to re-enter the room was to discover it in ruins, the windows broken, the gale howling in, snow piling up on the sofa and chairs. It was something Mark should have known, could have predicted, but had tried to ignore the weekend he met Robert and found the door so easy to open. Saturday evening had passed and he had managed to say nothing, to tell Carl only that he had gone window-shopping in Oxford Street and brought nothing home, but on Sunday afternoon as he hurried from Knightsbridge to meet Carl at the pub he knew that he would tell him about Robert, that the habit of talking about everything, of keeping nothing from him, was stronger than the wisdom of silence. Perhaps, too, confession would become exorcism or cure; if he admitted what had happened, exposed it to the heat of Carl's temper, he might see his desire for Robert, the dryness in his mouth and the tautness in his stomach, fade like a film exposed to light, leaving him free to try again with Carl, to bring back the excitement and enthusiasm that had long since died.

He was late; Carl, waiting at the pub door, accepted his apology with a smile of forgiveness. 'How was it?' Mark asked as they walked in the direction of the tube.

'We were busy,' Carl said.

'What was the entertainment?'

'A country singer. She's new. She wasn't very good.'

'How's Jack?' The manager.

'O.K.'

There was a silence somewhere between the warm intimacy of lovers and the coldness of strangers forced to share a room, share a bed.

'I met someone interesting today.' Mark tried to make the comment trivial.

'Who?'

'A dancer.'

'Where?'

'In Hyde Park.'

'You were cruising.' The comment was flat.

'I wasn't. I don't even think he's gay.'

Carl said nothing, showed neither belief nor curiosity. Mark was irritated, wanted his revelation to force some kind of catharsis, of confrontation.

'You should meet him.'

'Why?'

'You might like him.'

Again silence.

'I may be seeing him on Tuesday. Come along.'

'I have to work.'

'Then another time.'

They walked down into the tube station and waited for their train, saying nothing, having nothing to say. In the carriage they say opposite each other, Carl with one arm along the back of the seat, the other resting in his lap. Mark wished he was carrying something, something to hold, something to distract him from Carl's stare. He felt as if he was being watched by a detective seeking signs of guilt, evidence of a crime that had not been committed, as if the set of his mouth and eyes betrayed only his desire for Robert and not his love for Carl. Or perhaps what Carl was seeing, what was holding his attention, was a confusion so great Mark himself shied away from it, a conflict not merely between his heart and his reason but within them both. All he wanted was Carl as a lover and Robert as a friend – a friend with whom he might freely go out and sleep – but the more he let himself acknowledge that apparently so simple and so innocuous wish, the more disturbed and unhappy he felt.

'You don't have to come with me,' Carl interrupted his thoughts.

'To Charles's? Why shouldn't I?'

'You hardly know him.'

Carl shrugged.

What's wrong, Mark wanted to ask. He wanted to go over and shake Carl's shoulders, force that expression of distance and unconcern to break into tears or anger. If he had done so he might have precipitated the argument, the shouting and the accusations that were to come later; then Mark might have understood, as abruptly and as violently as a blow to the gut that his meeting Robert, his longing for Robert was not a bad habit that would be frowned on, but was as fatal to his life with Carl as if one of them in a moment of madness had slipped poison into the other's drink. If he had insisted then, in the shaking and rattling train, that Carl bring up his anger, his disgust, confront him with the fact that deep and strong emotions could neither be manipulated nor ignored, if Carl had stated quite calmly that should Mark ever meet this dancer again even for a chaste drink in a bar, a chaperoned stroll through the National Gallery, he, Carl, would without further comment leave, then that quiet threat, that reminder of Carl's self-respect, might have shocked Mark into forgetting Robert, into never meeting him again, into remembering where his loyalties lay.

Perhaps. It was more likely that in such a public place all that would have developed would have been an argument of the type that had come between them before, where neither confessed what he really wanted or was afraid of, where the situation was so wrapped up in potentialities and hypotheses that each could pretend that nothing had changed, that their recurring squabbling was temporary, like a bumpy stretch of road which would soon give way to smooth tarmac again. So Mark said nothing, hoped that Carl's mood would pass, resolved to keep silent about Robert and hoped vaguely that the situation would work itself out, that he would lose nothing, perhaps only shift emphasis in his relationships as if he were settling more comfortably into an old and unevenly stuffed chair.

157

For the rest of that day and all of the next he wondered whether he should phone Robert, should cancel the date they had made for Tuesday or insist that it be changed to a time when Carl could come with him. He should, he knew, call while Carl was there, show that there was nothing to hide, that Robert was no closer to him than Charles whom they had visited the day before, yet he was afraid that with Carl in the room and Robert at the end of the line his words and self-assurance would fail him. He would sound to the one dishonest and untrustworthy, to the other bumbling and foolish, and he would put down the receiver to find that he had lost the confidence of both. When he did ring, on Monday evening while Carl was at work, intent on resolving the situation, on telling Robert everything that he had so far not revealed, it was to hear endless, unanswered ringing and to realise that the next day, however stupid the action might be, they would meet alone together as planned.

Mark had been as apprehensive the evening he had rung Gene. He had known that morning when the letter arrived what it contained. He had stuffed it into his pocket as he walked out on his way to school, had sat in the underground, aware of it and afraid to take it out, to have his suspicions confirmed. The later he looked at it, he told himself, the less it would affect him; the contents would not change, but their power to hurt would be softened, blunted by the passing of time. The morning routine, the demands of his timetable and of the students, helped him to forget at least temporarily that Gene had written, but at lunchtime, with forty blank minutes ahead of him, he knew that the letter would have to be opened, that he had to see in reality what he already knew in imagination. For privacy he sat in the toilet like one of his pupils smoking, his eyes rushing over the thin letters with their erratic loops which told him that Gene did not want him to come back, that he was seeing someone else, that he hoped Mark understood. He read the pages again, slowly, hoping that in his haste he had missed a line, a phrase, a word that would somehow negate the rest of

158

the letter, make it no more than a hypothesis, a possibility that Gene had considered but rejected. There was nothing however, only the starkness of brief explanation. 'The day after you left I met François. He is studying languages and hopes to be an interpreter. We get on very well together. I know this must hurt you and I wish I could do it in some other way. But it wouldn't have worked out between us and it wasn't fair on you coming over every month.' But I wanted to come over, Mark shouted silently at the paper in his hands as if it could carry his words back to Gene. I would have come over every weekend if I had to and chucked in my job and got one in Paris and I could have lived with you and we could have got a bigger apartment and it could have worked . . .

He had sat there wanting to cry and, unable to, the emotion built up like a headache until he found himself looking at his watch. He saw the time, put the letter back in his pocket and got up to leave. What seemed strangest in this situation was the fact that he knew he was about to go back into class, that he knew he would teach this afternoon as efficiently, if not as enthusiastically, as he usually did, that he was not hysterical, that on the worst day of his life he could carry on as if nothing had happened, as if he were the same person he had always been rather than someone whose whole reason for living had been swept aside, who was now alone, who would always be alone. Perhaps there was something wrong with him; perhaps the shock was delayed and he would find himself suddenly and at the most inopportune moment collapsing into tears, oblivious of whoever was around, whether it was his pupils or colleagues or passers-by who stopped to stare in the street.

He did not, however, collapse; at school behaved only as if he indeed had a headache for the rest of the day and returned home – to the flat from which he would shortly be moving – at the same time as he always did. He spent an hour in front of the television absorbed by cartoons and children's quiz programmes until it occurred to him that he could at least phone Gene, could try to make him change his mind, show him that the person

159

he had rejected, the insecure wimp, had gone, had been replaced by a stronger, more confident Mark he would not be ashamed to have as his lover. Besides, they barely knew each other, they were at the start of a relationship; it was wrong, unfair, stupid to call a halt now, to say that something would not work when they had barely given it a chance.

He read the letter again, saw no traps, no double meanings, no opportunities for misunderstanding. He spread it out on the table beside the phone, checked Gene's number and the code for Paris and dialled, aware of the nervous beating of his heart, of the coldness under his arms and the dryness of his mouth.

'Hallo.' The familiar, distant accent.

'Gene. It's Mark.'

'Oh.'

There may have been a pause but Mark let it pass. 'I got your letter.'

This time there was silence. 'I'm sorry I had to let you know that way,' Gene said at last, 'but I couldn't let you come back. It wouldn't be right.'

'Why not?'

'Because I couldn't see you. I mean you couldn't stay here.'

'Because of François?'

'Yes.'

'I could stay in a hotel.' He was clutching at straws.

'And what would you do?'

'See you when you were free.'

'But I might not be free.'

There was no leeway, no point in Gene's words where Mark could find access, could lever an opening, lever his way back into Gene's life.

'Mark, I'm sorry,' Gene went on. 'It wouldn't have worked.'

'Why not?' The question was a reflex; he knew the answer, every aspect of it.

'Because you live in London.'

'I could move to Paris.'

'We're different people.'

'I'm not the person I used to be. I've changed.'

Again there was silence. Gene seemed to have nothing to say and everything Mark said seemed to have no effect.

'I mean, I could understand,' Mark went on, 'if we'd been through a relationship, if it hadn't worked out, but this is only the beginning. We should ' – you must – 'give it a chance.'

'It would be no good, Mark.'

'Why?' All the anger and frustration would have spilled out in self-pity and tears if he had not been the new Mark now.

'It just wouldn't.'

'What's François like?' Mark asked after another pause.

'He's O.K.'

'Are you happy?'

'Yeah.' The voice was calm, emotionless.

'Can I come and see you sometime – as a friend?'

'Of course.'

'What about you coming to London?'

'I don't think so.'

'Why not?'

'Maybe one day.'

'I still think this is silly,' Mark said. 'I should be on the train this evening, pounding on your door first thing in the morning and shaking some sense into your head.' Gene said nothing. 'I'll miss you.' Again there was the threat of tears as he heard himself give up, resigned to the fact that he had lost Gene, that he had, if not tonight, the last time they met, let him slip through his fingers, never to be recovered.

'I'll miss you.' Perhaps Gene meant it.

'How's the painting?' Anything to keep talking, not to lose contact.

'The same.'

'Have you started on anything else?'

'No.'

'I haven't written anything either. I've had no time.' The casual tone sounded forced, a bad actor in a repertory play. He wondered if Gene was impatient to put the phone down, finally cut Mark out of his life.

'You should.'

'What?'

'Write something.'

'You won't reconsider?' This time his tone was genuinely light.

'Mark,' Gene warned.

'O.K. No harm in trying. I'd better go. Thanks for everything.'

'Thank you.'

'Bye.'

You bastard, Mark thought, hearing Gene's dying voice as he replaced the receiver. You fucking bastard. Just one more time and I would have proved to you that everything was all right, that we could make it. His chest suddenly trembled and he found himself crying as hard and as bitterly as he had earlier expected, his hands, after they brushed away the first tears, suddenly striking out at the nearest chair, hitting it not because it was Gene, nor because it was even himself, but simply because he had to hit something, express his anger and frustration in some way. Then he had heard the front door open, David or Mike or coming in, and he had to stop, to contain his emotions with the same difficulty and futility as replacing the cork in a champagne bottle, and pretend that his red face meant nothing, that everything was all right, that maybe the guy he'd been seeing in Paris had called it off, but it didn't matter, he'd been expecting it to finish; it saved time and money and it hadn't got far anyway.

Almost two years later he had returned to a different flat, one that he nominally owned, that he shared with a lover who had been working all evening, serving drinks, washing glasses, counting change, making jokes, watching the clock, while he, Mark, had been lying on the bed of a small Soho flat, staring down at, touching, making love to a nineteen-year-old dancer whom for the past three days he had been unable to get out of his mind. Everything was as he had left it, each piece of furniture stolidly in its place, each ornament unmoved, each picture unchanged. The bed had been made that morning; the

162

mugs waiting in the kitchen to be washed had been there since the afternoon; his briefcase lay half-open on the sofa where he had dropped it on his return from school. He had expected these inanimate objects to betray him, to reveal somehow that they knew where he had been and what he had done, but they stood motionless and silent, staring at him with a disapproval that only he could read. Relieved yet restless, he pottered in the kitchen, washing dishes, tidying up, wiping surfaces, then went to sit in the living-room, watching television until Carl came home.

Soon, however, he realised that if he were sitting here when Carl returned, if they met face to face, he would not be able to conceal what he had done; the moment and the emotions that had accompanied it were too recent, too intense to be buried under the thin patina of routine greeting. Carl would only have to look at him to see the hesitancy, the unexpected and inexplicable change, and the evening would be dragged out of him before he had time to understand it, to decide whether Robert could be, if not forgotten, at least pushed aside or whether the half-hour they had spent making love had to be repeated at whatever cost to himself and Carl. He stood, switched off the set, and went through to the bathroom, where he cleaned his teeth and stared at his reflection in the mirror as if not the A of adultery but some more subtle, modern sign of what he had done was emblazoned on his brow. He saw no change, but he also hardly recognised the individual who looked back at him; each feature taken separately was familiar, but together they were hostile to each other, refused to assemble into the person he had once been.

He lay in bed in the dark, eyes open, wide awake, his body still but his mind trembling as from flu or some fever. It was only the click of the front door that calmed him, and listening to Carl moving quietly through the flat, the switching on and off of lights measuring and announcing his path. Finally the bedroom door was pushed open and he tiptoed in, halting by the chair to remove each shoe, pull off his shirt, unzip and let his trousers drop to the floor.

163

He could pretend to be asleep, and postpone talking to Carl until the morning when awkwardness and abruptness could be blamed on the need to get dressed and to work on time, but such action would be dishonest, as much of a betrayal as the time he had spent with Robert. So, his voice loud in the stillness, he announced as he felt Carl get into bed beside him, 'I'm awake, you know.'

'I thought you were.' Carl stretched out, let one leg rest on Mark's, an arm curve over his shoulder.

'The evening go O.K.?'

'Yeah. What about you?'

'Mm.'A light, careless sound. 'I had a drink with that guy I told you about.'

'The dancer?'

'Yes.'

Carl was silent, then quietly asked, 'Did you sleep with him?'

What makes you think that, he could ask, buying himself time. He could lie, knowing that Carl trusted him, that he would, despite himself, accept the statement and go to sleep. But it was because Carl trusted him, because he had never lied, that he could not lie now, that he could never lie to him. 'Yes.'

There was a moment of silence, of stillness, then without warning Carl's voice lacerated him: 'You bastard!' His calf was struck by Carl's foot. The shock, the violent anger in place of sullen mood, was greater than the pain and was immediately compounded by Carl's fist hitting his back and more words, distinct only in rage, insulting, attacking, tearing at him.

This isn't happening, Mark told himself as, pulling back from Carl's buffets, he found himself falling from the bed and getting to his feet with difficulty, followed by Carl shouting 'You promised! You promised! You promised!' as he hit out blindly. This is stupid, ridiculous, the two of us naked, sparring like drunken and incompetent boxers, or rather Carl fighting while I try to defend myself. It occurred to Mark to hit back, but he could never strike Carl, never even in anger; all he could do was try to

164

restrain him, to hold his arms until he calmed down. 'Stop it,' he said. 'This is childish, ridiculous.' But Carl's only response was to continue his flailing and to shout, to wail, 'I did everything for you, everything, everything!'

The flash of truth and guilt that struck Mark was more painful than any of Carl's blows. The sentiment that he was in the right, the righteous pride that he did not lower himself to violence was swept aside by the realisation that all that was happening now was his fault, his responsibility. If he could only apologise . . . But Carl's rage was not diminishing; only the litany had changed. 'Get out! Get out!! GET OUT!'

'Carl . . .'

'GET OUT!!!'

Mark's presence was only fuel for further explosion. Reluctantly he moved towards the door, holding Carl, hoping that at any moment the storm would abate, the voice would die, the tears would deepen into sobs and, into the void, into the silence, he could beg Carl's forgiveness and together they could begin, slowly, carefully, delicately, to start all over again. It did not happen. The door opened, and Carl found the strength to break free, push Mark through and slam it after him, creating the silence Mark had wanted and the separation he feared. He stood alone in the hall, trembling, almost in shock, listening for Carl but hearing no movement. 'I'm sorry,' he said no more loudly than was necessary to be heard on the other side of the door. There was no reply. 'I'm sorry,' he repeated more loudly, reaching out and starting to turn the handle.

'GO AWAY!'

Mark stood for a moment, aware of both sorrow and rage, but his mind was otherwise blank, drained of thoughts and emotion. He realised, without quite knowing why, that he did not want to go back into that room and so he went to the one adjacent, the one that was nominally Carl's and was unused, empty and cold. There he crawled into the bed and covered himself with its few blankets; there were no sheets but he neither cared nor knew where to find them if he should want them. His eyes closed and he was aware of little more than words that he repeated over and over

165

without quite understanding either their context or their meaning. 'What have I done? What have I done? What have I done?' If he slept it was briefly, lightly, sinking momentarily into dreams where people he knew but could not identify attacked him or fled him as he stood helpless, pinned to the ground by something he could not see. In the longer, waking moments, his thoughts slowly came together again, but his emotions, however, still floated out of reach and he lay numb, staring into the gloom at the ceiling as if there he could see the memory of how he had loved and been loved, hurt and been happy. Every so often he looked at the bedside clock and saw that its hands moved more slowly than he thought possible, delaying beyond comprehension the moment when he might talk to Carl again, when he might understand and begin to sort out the mess he had made of their lives.

At six o'clock he got up and, conscious of a headache, of a dryness in his mouth and weakness in his stomach, went through to the kitchen to make the first coffee of the many that he knew would have to see him through the day. It was then, sitting at the table, staring out at the early morning light, that he saw clearly the awesome extent of his actions, that what he had done was not merely sleep with another, a sin in itself of little importance, but he had destroyed the whole basis of his relationship with Carl. 'I did everything for you! I did everything for you!' Carl had shouted at him, referring not to the fact that he willingly cooked and cleaned and washed up, but that he had changed his whole life, had stayed in London, given up drinking, given up his obsession with money and its attractions, given his all to Mark – so much more than Mark had ever given him. And Mark had taken that love casually, as thoughtlessly as if it were a book to read, a drink that had been thrust into his hands, and in having sex with Robert had shown it a contempt that only Mark deserved.

'Oh, God,' he thought and rested his head in his hands as tears welled up within him. Yet his eyes remained dry for, no matter how great his guilt, how great his sorrow for Carl, holding back the full expression of these

166

emotions was the thought of Robert, the excitement of knowing him, the longing to see him again. However much Mark tried to concentrate on his guilt and the pain of a few hours before, he was distracted by the insistent whisper, 'If you lose Carl there's Robert; if you lose Carl there's Robert, ' as tempting as the promise of an undiscoverable theft.

The door opened; Carl came in. 'Are you all right?' Mark asked.

'Don't talk to me.' Carl felt the kettle's weight, switched it on.

'We have to talk.'

Carl said nothing.

'Carl, I'm sorry.'

Carl poured water into a mug. 'Why? You wanted to fuck with him, so you fucked with him.'

'I'm sorry I hurt you.'

'If you're sorry, why did you do it?' The anger had gone; his voice was cold, uninterested, words uttered out of habit.

'I don't know.' But he did know, although he tried to ignore the answer, consider it irrelevant; Robert offered excitement, challenge, a sense of wonder, while life with Carl was narrowing to a dull and limited future.

Carl picked up his coffee and walked towards the door.

'If I promise never to do it again, can we forget it?' Mark asked, begged.

'But you will do it again.'

Yes, I probably will. 'Carl, I could have lied last night. You would have believed me. None of this would have happened; we would have carried on the same. I told you the truth because I love you. Can't you understand that? I love you.'

Carl stopped, turned. 'It's one of the things I loved about you,' he said, tears appearing at his eyes. 'You were the most honest person I knew. I trusted you.'

'You can still trust me.' Mark wanted to go over, put his arm round Carl, have him sit down, comfort him, but was afraid to do so, afraid to be rejected.

'I can trust you to break you word.'

167

'Carl . . .' He had gone. Mark hesitated, then stood up and went out into the hall, opened the bedroom door.

'Don't come in.'

'Carl . . .'

'DON'T COME IN!' The same anger and violence hung in his words as during the night. Mark moved away, wondering what to do as he shivered and realised he was naked and the hall was cold.

For an hour he watched television in the living-room covered by a blanket from the spare bed, allowing his mind to be dulled by the triviality of the early morning programme. Once he got up and knocked on the bedroom door, asking if he could go in, but Carl's voice, dry, cold, told him no. Eventually, when it became too late to do otherwise, he stood up, switched off the set and went to warn Carl that he had to enter, had to get ready for school. There was no reply. He pushed the door open and saw Carl lying in bed, his face turned to the wall. He went over and sat next to him, but Carl moved apart, told him to go away, to get his clothes and go. Mark stood, looked down at the body buried under the duvet as if it was trying to hide from the world and was aware once again of the extent, of the terrible damage, of what he had done. He suddenly realised that he, Mark, had been the stronger of the two, the one on whom responsibility for keeping them together lay. Carl had trusted him, had placed all his faith in him like a child handing over its most precious possession – only to see it swept carelessly aside and shatter on the ground. For a brief moment Mark hated himself with a violence as great as Carl's anger, hated himself for having hurt his lover, for having not the slightest idea of how he could repair the damage he had done. Time, however, was advancing and his emotion crumbled under the pressure to get dressed, to make himself presentable, to leave home, to leave Carl and go, without the slightest enthusiasm, to school.

'I'll see you tonight,' he said, when his jacket was on and his tie was straight. He leaned over to kiss Carl but the figure below him pulled away.

'Just go.'

168

'I'm sorry,' Mark repeated at the door, knowing that to Carl the words meant nothing, and knowing there was nothing more he could do.

The day's routine pulled him through the morning but with the lunchtime break came memory and guilt. He wanted to call Carl but remembered that he would be at work, would be neither free nor in the mood to hear Mark's self-justification. Instead, in the relative privacy of the staff phone, he dialled Robert's number without expecting him to reply. It was, however, Robert who answered, who listened without comment as Mark explained that he had problems at home, that he wanted to see Robert but could not, that he would call and tell him everything in a day or two. As Mark spoke he both dreaded and hoped that Robert would be as shocked and distant as Carl had been, that he would say that he did not want to meet anyone as dishonest and selfish as Mark, but when he came to the end he made no comment, uttered only platitudes that expressed neither pleasure nor anger. So Mark, with the option still open, the decision not made for him, could not prevent himself from repeating that he hoped it would all blow over soon, that he was missing Robert, that he hoped they would see each other again soon, that he would call immediately he could. But even those words did not draw from Robert the tenderness that Mark sought, the verbal expression of their love-making the previous evening, and Mark replaced the receiver wondering what was happening, what he was doing, whether he was about to throw away silver to discover that the gold coin that lured him was no more than a glint of light, a flash of sun.

He hurried home from school that afternoon to discover that Carl had gone, that his clothes and records and other belongings had been pulled from drawers and cupboards and stuffed into suitcases and cardboard boxes, a quick and careless exit that must have been made while Mark was pontificating in class, while he was taking a hurried and unwanted meal, while he was debating whether to phone. There was no note, only the key and photographs of Mark and the two of them together strewn across the

169

kitchen table in a mute gesture of contempt. Mark's first reaction was that running away was melodramatic and ridiculous, but that gave way almost immediately to the fear that Carl had indeed gone, had left as the result of a carefully considered decision, not a sudden, impetuous move. And if he had gone, then Mark would never see him again, for Carl had never given him any address; having lived together since they met there had never been cause to write, to arrange any other form of contact. It was then that Mark collapsed, that he sank into a chair and shook with sobs of deep unhappiness and anger, wondering how anyone could be as stupid, as selfish as he had been.

He had never heard from Carl again; the embarrassing and difficult phone calls to the bar, to friends and acquaintances only let him know that Carl had gone back to Lancashire, that the one person who had his address had promised neither to reveal it nor to pass on messages. He told himself he would wait for a week, allow Carl time to reconsider and return before calling Robert, but it was the next day he rang, cradling the phone, staring at the living-room door as if expecting Carl to come it. The pain of separation had swiftly dulled, anaesthetised by the excitement of Robert, and lingered on only as curiosity in idle moments as to where Carl was now, what he was doing. Yet even if he thought of him seldom, Mark knew he still loved Carl, still cared for him, hoped that wherever he was, whatever he was doing, whether he was on his own, with Edwin or some other, he was happy, that he remembered Mark with more affection than bitterness, and planned that one day they would meet again.

But Carl was in the past; on this quiet and warm Sunday evening when, even with the sounds of Ben now returned and cooking in the kitchen, he was alone. It was Robert he should be thinking of. Later that night, if all were well between them, if Mark's thoughtlessness had not lost him Robert as it had lost him Carl, Robert would call, would say he was at home, would tell him about the performances, would arrange to meet him the next day. And if he did not call, if it was Mark who

telephoned th...
still upset, still u...
what then? Did Ma...
who took offence so...
so important, created su... *learned that Robert was*
should drift apart with no... *tty gesture of the tape,*
where the danger lay. Where they... *olved with someone*
Robert's protestations, despite his patina... *mall matter were*
intelligence, in age and therefore outlook. Robe... *on them, they*
more than a teenager approaching his twentieth birth... *was not*
a talented and precocious individual perhaps, but one with *despite*
all the egocentricity and failings of youth. Everything that *and*
angered Mark, that upset or saddened him, could be
traced to that root; Robert's occasional failure to telephone
when he had promised, his insistence on going home
rather than staying with Mark, his refusal to move out,
to live with Mark or on his own all stemmed from the
fact that he was too young to commit himself, too young
to understand what commitment meant. He might have
told Mark that he loved him, even believed that he loved
him, but his actions, or his lack of actions suggested he
did not yet know what the word meant, suggested that for
him it was more a careless affection than a deep emotion,
the desire to have someone to call a lover rather than
uncompromising acceptance of the responsibilities that
love implied.

And if he was that young, if the ten years between
them was as great as any gap of generations, then Mark
was likely to be no more than a stage on Robert's route
of emotional discovery, one of a series of lovers, each
of whom would be in some way different from the
others and would, implicitly or explicitly, help him to
understand what he wanted from such affairs until, when
he was twenty-four, twenty-five, he would meet the man
he would whole-heartedly and unreservedly love. If Mark
believed that Robert was ready to settle, to give himself
to Mark or anyone now for the rest of his life, he was
fooling himself, was by imbuing the relationship with
such seriousness aiming for unhappiness again. He had
to accept that his relationship with Robert would not last,

row bored, find his
other's mind, another's
that the dancer sic or art or writing or dance.
attention taken what would be both easy and pain-
body, another himself alone again, with perhaps no
Then, after it's place as Robert had taken Carl's.
ful, Mark nt, initially depressing, faded into the under-
one to that his own situation differed from Robert's only
The
stge. If he was only a stage in Robert's life then Robert
was only a stage in his, as Gene had been, as Carl had
been, as all the others with whom he had spent a few days
or a few hours. He was only twenty-eight; should Robert
leave nothing would stop him from meeting another
man as handsome, as intelligent, as warm as Robert;
nothing would prevent him from falling in love again
and again and again. Unlike two years before when he
had padded round the sauna in search of something he
did not understand, Mark was worthy now to be loved;
no longer did he have any doubt that others would fall
for him, would find him attractive, find his presence both
interesting and entertaining. He had learned much more
than he had realised, learned that Gene, Carl and Robert,
the good times and the bad, were not the end but the
beginning, that whatever happened now, whether Robert
phoned today, tomorrow or never again was irrelevant.
From now on everything would go Mark's way, would
be experience from which he could only profit; quietly he
laughed to himself, happy, genuinely happy, for the first
time in his life.